3001

THE FINAL ODYSSEY

ARTHUR C. CLARKE

3001

THE FINAL ODYSSEY

BALLANTINE BOOKS   NEW YORK

A Del Rey® Book
Published by Ballantine Books

Copyright © 1997 by Arthur C. Clarke

Grateful acknowledgment is made to Henry Holt & Co., Inc., and The Society
of Authors, as the literary representative of the Estate of A. E. Housman, for
permission to reprint an excerpt from *The Collected Poems of A. E. Housman*.
Copyright © 1936 by Barclay Banks Ltd., © 1964 by Robert E. Symons.

ISBN 0-345-31522-7

Manufactured in the United States of America

For Cherene, Tamara, and Melinda—
May you be happy in a far better century than mine

CONTENTS

PROLOGUE: THE FIRSTBORN

Call them the Firstborn. Though they were not remotely human, they were flesh and blood, and when they looked out across the deeps of space, they felt awe, and wonder—and loneliness. As soon as they possessed the power, they began to seek for fellowship among the stars.

In their explorations, they encountered life in many forms, and watched the workings of evolution on a thousand worlds. They saw how often the first faint sparks of intelligence flickered and died in the cosmic night.

And because, in all the Galaxy, they had found nothing more precious than Mind, they encouraged its dawning everywhere. They became farmers in the fields of stars; they sowed, and sometimes they reaped.

And sometimes, dispassionately, they had to weed.

The great dinosaurs had long since passed away, their morning promise annihilated by a random hammerblow from space, when the survey ship entered the Solar System after a voyage that had already lasted a thousand years. It swept past the frozen outer planets, paused briefly above the deserts of dying Mars, and presently looked down on Earth.

Spread out beneath them, the explorers saw a world swarming with life. For years they studied, collected, catalogued. When they had learned all that they could, they began to modify. They tinkered with the destiny of many species, on land and in the seas. But which of their experiments would bear fruit, they could not know for at least a million years.

They were patient, but they were not yet immortal. There was so much to do in this universe of a hundred billion suns, and other worlds were calling. So they set out once more into the abyss, knowing that they would never come this way again. Nor was there any need: the servants they had left behind would do the rest.

On Earth, the glaciers came and went, while above them the changeless Moon still carried its secret from the stars. With a yet slower rhythm than the polar ice, the tides of civilization ebbed and flowed across the Galaxy. Strange and beautiful and terrible empires rose and fell, and passed on their knowledge to their successors.

And now, out among the stars, evolution was driving toward new goals. The first explorers of Earth had long since come to the limits of flesh and blood; as soon as their machines were better than their bodies, it was time to move. First their brains, and then their thoughts alone, they transferred into shining new homes of metal and gemstone. In these, they roamed the Galaxy. They no longer built spaceships. They were spaceships.

But the age of the Machine-entities swiftly passed. In their ceaseless experimenting, they had learned to store knowledge in the structure of space itself, and to preserve their thoughts for eternity in frozen lattices of light.

Into pure energy, therefore, they presently transformed themselves; and on a thousand worlds, the empty shells they had discarded twitched for a while in a mindless dance of death, then crumbled into dust.

Now they were Lords of the Galaxy, and could rove at will among the stars, or sink like a subtle mist through the very interstices of space. Though they were freed at last from the tyranny of matter, they had not wholly forgotten their origin, in the warm slime of a vanished sea. And their marvelous instruments still continued to function, watching over the experiments started so many ages ago.

But no longer were they always obedient to the mandates of their creators; like all material things, they were not immune to the corruptions of Time and its patient, unsleeping servant, Entropy.

And sometimes, they discovered and sought goals of their own.

I. STAR CITY

1. COMET COWBOY

Captain Dimitri Chandler [M2973.04.21/93.106//Mars//Space-Acad3005]—or "Dim" to his very best friends—was understandably annoyed. The message from Earth had taken six hours to reach the spacetug *Goliath*, here beyond the orbit of Neptune; if it had arrived ten minutes later he could have answered, "Sorry—can't leave now—we've just started to deploy the sunscreen."

The excuse would have been perfectly valid: wrapping a comet's core in a sheet of reflective film only a few molecules thick but kilometers on a side, was not the sort of job you could abandon while it was half-completed.

Still, it would be a good idea to obey this ridiculous request: he was already in disfavor Sunward, through no fault of his own. Collecting ice from the rings of Saturn and nudging it toward Venus and Mercury, where it was really needed, had started back in the 2700s—three centuries ago. Captain Chandler had never been able to see any real difference in the "before and after" images the Solar Conservers were always producing, to support their accusations of celestial vandalism. But the general public, still sensitive to the ecological disasters of previous centuries, had thought otherwise, and the "Hands off Saturn!" vote had passed by a substantial majority. As a result, Chandler was no longer a Ring Rustler, but a Comet Cowboy.

So here he was at an appreciable fraction of the distance to Alpha Centauri, rounding up stragglers from the Kuiper Belt. There was certainly enough ice out here to cover Mercury and Venus with oceans kilometers deep, but it might take centuries to extinguish their hellfires and make them suitable for life. The Solar Conservers, of course, were still protesting against this, though no longer with so much enthusiasm. The millions dead from the tsunami caused by the Pacific asteroid in 2304—how ironic that a land impact would have done much less damage!—had reminded all future generations that the human race had too many eggs in one fragile basket.

Well, Chandler told himself, it would be fifty years before this particular package reached its destination, so a delay of a week would hardly make much difference. But all the calculations about rotation, center of mass, and thrust vectors would have to be redone, and radioed back to Mars for checking. It was a good idea to do your sums carefully, before nudging billions of tons of ice along an orbit that might take it within hailing distance of Earth.

As they had done so many times before, Captain Chandler's eyes strayed toward the ancient photograph above his desk. It showed a three-masted steamship, dwarfed by the iceberg that was looming above it—as, indeed, *Goliath* was dwarfed at this very moment.

How incredible, he had often thought, that only one long lifetime spanned the gulf between this primitive *Discovery* and the ship that had carried the same name to Jupiter! And what would those long-ago Antarctic explorers have made of the view from his bridge?

They would certainly have been disoriented, for the wall of ice beside which *Goliath* was floating stretched both upward and downward as far as the eye could see. And it was strange-looking ice, wholly lacking the immaculate whites and blues of the frozen Polar seas. In fact, it looked dirty—as indeed it was. For only some 90 percent was water-ice: the rest was a witches' brew of carbon and sulfur compounds, most of them stable only at temperatures not far above absolute zero. Thawing them out could produce unpleasant surprises: as one astrochemist had famously remarked, "Comets have bad breath."

"Skipper to all personnel," Chandler announced. "There's been a slight change of program. We've been asked to delay operations, to investigate a target that Spaceguard radar has picked up."

"Any details?" somebody asked, when the chorus of groans over the ship's intercom had died away.

"Not many, but I gather it's another Millennium Committee project they've forgotten to cancel."

More groans: everyone had become heartily sick of all the events planned to celebrate the end of the 2000s. There had been a general sigh of relief when January 1, 3001, had passed uneventfully, and the human race could resume its normal activities.

"Anyway, it will probably be another false alarm, like the last one. We'll get back to work just as quickly as we can. Skipper out."

This was the third wild-goose chase, Chandler thought morosely, he'd been involved with during his career. Despite centuries of exploration, the Solar System could still produce surprises, and presumably Spaceguard had a good reason for its request. He only hoped that some imaginative idiot hadn't once again sighted the fabled Golden Asteroid. If it did exist—which Chandler did not for a moment believe—it would be no more than a mineralogical curiosity: it would be of far less real value than the ice he was nudging Sunward, to bring life to barren worlds.

There was one possibility, however, which he did take quite seriously. Already, the human race had scattered its robot probes through a volume of space a hundred light-years across—and the Tycho Monolith was sufficient reminder that much older civilizations had engaged in similar activities. There might well be other alien artifacts in the Solar System, or in transit through it. Captain Chandler suspected that Spaceguard had something like this in mind: otherwise it would hardly have diverted a Class I spacetug to go chasing after an unidentified radar blip.

Five hours later, the questing *Goliath* detected the echo at extreme range; even allowing for the distance, it seemed disappointingly small. However, as it grew clearer and stronger, it began to give the signature of a metallic object, perhaps a couple of meters long. It was traveling on an orbit heading out of the Solar System, so was almost certainly, Chandler´ decided, one of the myriad pieces of space-junk that Mankind had tossed toward the stars during the last millennium—and which might one day provide the only evidence that the human race had ever existed.

Then it came close enough for visual inspection, and Captain Chandler realized, with awed astonishment, that some patient historian was still checking the earliest records of the Space Age. What a pity that the computers had given him the answer, just a few years too late for the Millennium celebrations!

"*Goliath* here," Chandler radioed Earthward, his voice tinged with pride as well as solemnity. "We're bringing aboard a thousand-year-old astronaut. And I can guess who it is."

2. AWAKENING

Frank Poole awoke, but he did not remember. He was not even sure of his name.

Obviously, he was in a hospital room: even though his eyes were still closed, the most primitive, and evocative, of his senses told him that. Each breath brought the faint and not unpleasant tang of antiseptics in the air, and it triggered a memory of the time when—of course!—as a reckless teenager he had broken a rib in the Arizona Hang-Gliding Championship.

Now it was all beginning to come back. I'm Deputy Commander Frank Poole, Executive Officer, USSS *Discovery*, on a Top Secret mission to Jupiter—

It seemed as if an icy hand had gripped his heart. He remembered, in slow-motion playback, that runaway space-pod jetting toward him, metal claws outstretched. Then the silent impact—and the not-so-silent hiss of air rushing out of his suit. After that—one last memory, of spinning helplessly in space, trying in vain to reconnect his broken air-hose.

Well, whatever mysterious accident had happened to the space-pod controls, he was safe now. Presumably Dave had made a quick EVA and rescued him before lack of oxygen could do permanent brain damage.

Good old Dave! he told himself. I must thank—just a moment!—I'm obviously not aboard *Discovery* now—surely I haven't been unconscious long enough to be taken back to Earth!

His confused train of thought was abruptly broken by the arrival of a Matron and two nurses, wearing the immemorial uniform of their profession. They seemed a little surprised: Poole wondered if he had awakened ahead of schedule, and the idea gave him a childish feeling of satisfaction.

"Hello!" he said, after several attempts; his vocal cords appeared to be very rusty. "How am I doing?"

Matron smiled back at him and gave an obvious "Don't try to talk" command by putting a finger to her lips. Then the two nurses fussed swiftly over him with practiced skill, checking pulse, temperature, reflexes. When one of them lifted his right arm and let it drop again, Poole noticed something peculiar. It fell slowly, and did not seem to weigh as much as normal. Nor, for that matter, did his body, when he attempted to move.

So I must be on a planet, he thought. Or a space station with artificial gravity. Certainly not Earth—I don't weigh enough.

He was about to ask the obvious question when Matron pressed something against the side of his neck, he felt a slight tingling sensation, and sank back into a dreamless sleep. Just before he became unconscious, he had time for one more puzzled thought.

How odd—they never spoke a single word—all the time they were with me.

3. REHABILITATION

When he woke again, and found Matron and nurses standing round his bed, Poole felt strong enough to assert himself.

"Where am I? Surely you can tell me that!"

The three women exchanged glances, obviously uncertain what to do next. Then Matron answered, enunciating her words very slowly and carefully: "Everything is fine, Mr. Poole. Professor Anderson will be here in a minute . . . He will explain."

Explain what? thought Poole with some exasperation. But at least she speaks English, even though I can't place her accent . . .

Anderson must have been already on his way, for the door opened moments later—to give Poole a brief glimpse of a small crowd of inquisitive onlookers peering in at him. He began to feel like a new exhibit at a zoo.

Professor Anderson was a small, dapper man whose features seemed to have combined key aspects of several races—Chinese, Polynesian, Nordic—in a thoroughly confusing fashion. He greeted Poole by holding up his right palm, then did an obvious double take and shook hands, with such a curious hesitation that he might have been rehearsing some quite unfamiliar gesture.

"Glad to see you're looking so well, Mr. Poole . . . We'll have you up in no time."

Again that odd accent and slow delivery—but the confident bedside manner was that of all doctors, in all places and all ages.

"I'm glad to hear it. Now perhaps you can answer a few questions . . ."

"Of course, of course. But just a minute."

Anderson spoke so rapidly and quietly to the Matron that Poole could catch only a few words, several of which were wholly unfamiliar to him. Then the Matron nodded at one of the nurses, who opened a wall cupboard and produced a slim metal band, which she proceeded to wrap around Poole's head.

"What's that for?" he asked—being one of those difficult patients, so annoying to doctors, who always want to know just what's happening to them. "EEG readout?"

Professor, Matron, and nurses looked equally baffled. Then a slow smile spread across Anderson's face.

"Oh—electro . . . enceph . . . alo . . . gram," he said slowly, as if dredging the word up from the depth of memory. "You're quite right. We just want to monitor your brain functions."

My brain would function perfectly well if you'd let me use it, Poole grumbled silently. *But at least we seem to be getting somewhere— finally.*

"Mr. Poole," said Anderson, still speaking in that curiously stilted voice, as if venturing in a foreign language, "you know, of course, that you were—disabled—in a serious accident, while you were working outside *Discovery*."

Poole nodded agreement.

"I'm beginning to suspect," he said dryly, "that 'disabled' is a slight understatement."

Anderson relaxed visibly, and a slow smile spread across his face.

"You're quite correct. Tell me what you think happened."

"Well, the best-case scenario is that, after I became unconscious, Dave Bowman rescued me and brought me back to the ship. How is Dave? No one will tell me anything!"

"All in due course . . . and the worst case?"

It seemed to Frank Poole that a chill wind was blowing gently on the back of his neck. The suspicion that had been slowly forming in his mind began to solidify.

"That I died, but was brought back here—wherever 'here' is—and you've been able to revive me. Thank you . . ."

"Quite correct. And you're back on Earth. Well, very near it."

What did he mean by "very near it"? There was certainly a gravity field here—so he was probably inside the slowly turning wheel of an orbiting space station. No matter: there was something much more important to think about.

Poole did some quick mental calculations. If Dave had put him in the hibernaculum, revived the rest of the crew, and completed the mission to Jupiter—why, he could have been "dead" for as much as five years!

"Just what date is it?" he asked, as calmly as possible.

Professor and Matron exchanged glances. Again Poole felt that cold wind on his neck.

"I must tell you, Mr. Poole, that Bowman did not rescue you. He believed—and we cannot blame him—that you were irrevocably dead. Also, he was facing a desperately serious crisis that threatened his own survival . . .

"So you drifted on into space, passed through the Jupiter system, and headed out toward the stars. Fortunately, you were so far below the freezing point that there was no metabolism—but it's a near-miracle that you were ever found at all. You are one of the luckiest men alive. No—ever to have lived!"

Am I? Poole asked himself bleakly. Five years, indeed! It could be a century—or even more.

"Let me have it," he demanded.

Professor and Matron seemed to be consulting an invisible monitor: when they looked at each other and nodded agreement, Poole guessed that they were all plugged into the hospital information circuit, linked to the headband he was wearing.

"Frank," said Professor Anderson, making a smooth switch to the role of longtime family physician, "this will be a great shock to you, but you're capable of accepting it—and the sooner you know, the better.

"We're near the beginning of the Fourth Millennium. Believe me—you left Earth almost a thousand years ago."

"I believe you," Poole answered calmly. Then, to his great annoyance, the room started to spin around him, and he knew nothing more.

When he regained consciousness, he found that he was no longer in a bleak hospital room but in a luxurious suite with attractive—and steadily changing—images on the walls. Some of them were famous and familiar paintings, others showed land- and seascapes that might have been from his own time. There was nothing alien or upsetting—that, he guessed, would come later.

His present surroundings had obviously been carefully programmed: he wondered if there was the equivalent of a television screen somewhere (how many channels would the Third Millennium have?) but could see no sign of any controls near his bed. There was so much he would have to learn in this new world: he was a savage who had suddenly encountered civilization.

But first, he must regain his strength—and learn the language; not even the advent of sound recording, already more than a century old when Poole was born, had prevented major changes in grammar and pronunciation. And there were thousands of new words, mostly from science and technology, though often he was able to make a shrewd guess at their meaning.

More frustrating, however, were the myriads of famous and infamous personal names that had accumulated over the millennium, and which meant nothing to him. For weeks, until he had built up a data bank, most of his conversations had to be interrupted with potted biographies.

As Poole's strength increased, so did the number of his visitors, though always under Professor Anderson's watchful eye. They included medical specialists, scholars of several disciplines, and—of the greatest interest to him—spacecraft commanders.

There was little that he could tell the doctors and historians that was not recorded somewhere in mankind's gigantic data banks, but he was often able to give them shortcuts and new insights about the events of his own time. Though they all treated him with the utmost respect and listened patiently as he tried to answer their questions, they seemed reluctant to answer his. Poole began to feel that he was being overprotected from culture shock, and half-seriously wondered how he could escape from his suite. On the few occasions he was alone, he was not surprised to discover that the door was locked.

Then the arrival of Dr. Indra Wallace changed everything. Despite her name, her chief racial component appeared to be Japanese, and there were times when with just a little imagination Poole could picture her as a rather mature Geisha Girl. It was hardly an appropriate image for a distinguished historian, holding a Virtual Chair at a university still boasting real ivy. She was the first visitor with a fluent command of Poole's own English, so he was delighted to meet her.

"Mr. Poole," she began, in a very businesslike voice, "I've been appointed your official guide and—let's say—mentor. My qualifications—I've specialized in your period—my thesis was 'The Collapse of the Nation-State, 2000–50.' I believe we can help each other in many ways."

"I'm sure we can. First I'd like you to get me out of here, so I can see a little of your world."

"Exactly what we intend to do. But first we must give you an Ident. Until then you'll be—what was the term?—a nonperson. It would be almost impossible for you to go anywhere, or get anything done. No input device would recognize your existence."

"Just what I expected," Poole answered, with a wry smile. "It was starting to get that way in my own time—and many people hated the idea."

"Some still do. They go off and live in the wilderness—there's a lot more on Earth than there was in your century! But they always take their compaks with them, so they can call for help as soon as they get into trouble. The median time is about five days."

"Sorry to hear that. The human race has obviously deteriorated."

He was cautiously testing her, trying to find the limits of her tolerance and to map out her personality. It was obvious that they were going to spend much time together, and that he would have to depend upon her in hundreds of ways. Yet he was still not sure if he would even like her: perhaps she regarded him merely as a fascinating museum exhibit.

Rather to Poole's surprise, she agreed with his criticism.

"That may be true—in some respects. Perhaps we're physically weaker, but we're healthier and better adjusted than most humans who have ever lived. The Noble Savage was always a myth."

She walked over to a small rectangular plate, set at eye level in the door. It was about the size of one of the countless magazines that had proliferated in the far-off Age of Print, and Poole had noticed that every room seemed to have at least one. Usually they were blank, but sometimes they contained lines of slowly scrolling text, completely meaningless to Poole even when most of the words were familiar. Once a plate in his suite had emitted urgent beepings, which he had ignored on the assumption that someone else would deal with the problem, whatever it was. Fortunately the noise stopped as abruptly as it had started.

Dr. Wallace laid the palm of her hand upon the plate, then removed it after a few seconds. She glanced at Poole, and said smilingly, "Come and look at this."

The inscription that had suddenly appeared made a good deal of sense, when he read it slowly:

WALLACE, INDRA [F2970.03.11/31.885//HIST.OXFORD]

"I suppose it means Female, date of birth March 11, 2970—and that you're associated with the Department of History at Oxford. And I guess that 31.885 is a personal identification number. Correct?"

"Excellent, Mr. Poole. I've seen some of your e-mail addresses and credit card numbers—hideous strings of alpha-numeric gibberish that no one could possibly remember! But we all know our date of birth, and not more than 99,999 other people will share it. So a five-figure number is all you'll ever need . . . and even if you forget that, it doesn't really matter. As you see, it's a part of you."

"Implant?"

"Yes—nanochip at birth, one in each palm for redundancy. You won't even feel yours when it goes in. But you've given us a small problem . . ."

"What's that?"

"The readers you'll meet most of the time are too simpleminded to believe your date of birth. So, with your permission, we've moved it up a thousand years."

"Permission granted. And the rest of the Ident?"

"Optional. You can leave it empty, give your current interests and location—or use it for personal messages, global or targeted."

Some things, Poole was quite sure, would not have changed over the centuries. A high proportion of those "targeted" messages would be very personal indeed.

He wondered if there were still self- or state-appointed censors in this day and age—and if their efforts at improving other people's morals had been more successful than in his own time.

He would have to ask Dr. Wallace about that, when he got to know her better.

4. A ROOM WITH A VIEW

"Frank—Professor Anderson thinks you're strong enough to go for a little walk."

"I'm very pleased to hear it. Do you know the expression 'stir crazy'?"

"No—but I can guess what it means."

Poole had so adapted to the low gravity that the long strides he was taking seemed perfectly normal. Half a gee, he had estimated—just right to give a sense of well-being. They met only a few people on their walk, all of them strangers, but every one gave a smile of recognition. By now, Poole told himself with a trace of smugness, I must be one of the best-known celebrities in this world. That should be a great help—when I decide what to do with the rest of my life. At least another century, if I can believe Anderson . . .

The corridor along which they were walking was completely featureless apart from occasional numbered doors, each bearing one of the universal recog panels. Poole had followed Indra for perhaps two hundred meters when he came to a sudden halt, shocked because he had not realized something so blindingly obvious.

"This space station must be enormous!" he exclaimed.

Indra smiled back at him.

"Didn't you have a saying—'You ain't seen anything yet'?"

" 'Nothing,' " he corrected, absentmindedly. He was still trying to estimate the scale of this structure when he had another surprise. Who would have imagined a space station large enough to boast a subway—admittedly a miniature one, with a single small coach capable of seating only a dozen passengers.

"Observation Lounge Three," ordered Indra, and they drew silently and swiftly away from the terminal.

Poole checked the time on the elaborate wristband whose functions he was still exploring. One minor surprise had been that the whole world was now on Universal Time: the confusing patchwork of Time Zones had been swept away by the advent of global communications. There had been much talk of this, back in the Twenty-first Century, and it had even been suggested that Solar should be replaced by Sidereal Time. Then, during the course of the year, the sun would move right round the clock, setting at the time it had risen six months earlier.

However, nothing had come of this "Equal time in the sun" proposal—or of even more vociferous attempts to reform the calendar. That particular job, it had been cynically suggested, would have to wait for somewhat major advances in technology. Someday, surely, one of God's minor mistakes would be corrected, and the Earth's orbit would be adjusted, to give every year twelve months of thirty exactly equal days . . .

As far as Poole could judge by speed and elapsed time, they must have traveled at least three kilometers before the vehicle came to a silent stop, the doors opened, and a bland autovoice intoned, "Have a good view. Thirty-five percent cloud cover today."

At last, thought Poole, we're getting near the outer wall. But here was another mystery—despite the distance he had gone, neither the strength nor the direction of gravity had altered! He could not imagine a spinning space station so huge that the gee-vector would not be changed by such a displacement . . . Could he really be on some planet after all? But he would feel lighter—usually much lighter—on any other habitable world in the Solar System.

When the outer door of the terminal opened, and Poole found himself entering a small airlock, he realized that he must indeed be in space. But where were the spacesuits? He looked around anxiously: it was against all his instincts to be so close to vacuum, naked and unprotected. One experience of that was enough . . .

"We're nearly there," said Indra reassuringly.

The last door opened, and he was looking out into the utter blackness of space, through a huge window that was curved both vertically and horizontally. He felt like a goldfish in its bowl, and hoped that the designers of this audacious piece of engineering knew exactly what they were doing. They certainly possessed better structural materials than had existed in his time.

Though the stars must be shining out there, his light-adapted eyes could see nothing but black emptiness beyond the curve of the great window. As he started to walk toward it to get a wider view, Indra restrained him and pointed straight ahead.

"Look carefully," she said. "Don't you see it?"

Poole blinked, and stared into the night. Surely it must be an illusion—even, heaven forbid, a crack in the window!

He moved his head from side to side. No, it was real. But what could it be? He remembered Euclid's definition: "A line has length, but no thickness."

For spanning the whole height of the window, and obviously continuing out of sight above and below, was a thread of light quite easy to see when he looked for it, yet so one-dimensional that the word "thin" could not even be applied. However, it was not completely featureless: there were barely visible spots of greater brilliance at irregular intervals along its length, like drops of water on a spider's web.

Poole continued walking toward the window, and the view expanded until at last he could see what lay below him. It was familiar enough; the whole continent of Europe, and much of northern Africa, just as he had seen them many times from space. So he was in orbit after all—probably an equatorial one, at a height of at least a thousand kilometers.

Indra was looking at him with a quizzical smile.

"Go closer to the window," she said, very softly. "So that you can look straight down. I hope you have a good head for heights."

What a silly thing to say to an astronaut! Poole told himself as he moved forward. If I ever suffered from vertigo, I wouldn't be in this business . . .

The thought had barely passed through his mind when he cried "My God!" and involuntarily stepped back from the window. Then, bracing himself, he dared to look again.

He was looking down on the distant Mediterranean from the face of a cylindrical tower, whose gently curving wall indicated a diameter of several kilometers. But that was nothing compared with its length, for it tapered away down, down, down—until it disappeared into the mists somewhere over Africa. He assumed that it continued all the way to the surface.

"How high are we?" he whispered.

"Two thousand kay. But now look upward."

This time, it was not such a shock: he had expected what he would see. The tower dwindled away until it became a glittering thread against the blackness of space, and he did not doubt that it continued all the way to the geostationary orbit, thirty-six thousand kilometers above the equator. Such fantasies had been well known in Poole's day: he had never dreamed he would see the reality—and be living in it.

He pointed toward the distant thread reaching up from the eastern horizon.

"That must be another one."

"Yes—the Asian Tower. We must look exactly the same to them."

"How many are there?"

"Just four, equally spaced around the Equator. Africa, Asia, America, Pacifica. The last one's almost empty—only a few hundred levels completed. Nothing to see except water . . ."

Poole was still absorbing this stupendous concept when a disturbing thought occurred to him.

"There were already thousands of satellites, at all sorts of altitudes, in my time. How do you avoid collisions?"

Indra looked slightly embarrassed.

"You know—I never thought about that—it's not my field." She paused for a moment, clearly searching her memory. Then her face brightened.

"I believe there was a big cleanup operation, centuries ago. There just aren't any satellites, below the stationary orbit."

That made sense, Poole told himself. They wouldn't be needed— the four gigantic towers could provide all the facilities once provided by thousands of satellites and space stations.

"And there have never been any accidents—any collisions with spaceships leaving Earth, or reentering the atmosphere?"

Indra looked at him with surprise.

"But they don't, anymore." She pointed to the ceiling. "All the spaceports are where they should be—up there, on the outer ring. I believe it's four hundred years since the last rocket lifted off from the surface of the Earth."

Poole was still digesting this when a trivial anomaly caught his attention. His training as an astronaut had made him alert to anything out of the ordinary: in space, that might be a matter of life or death.

The sun was out of view, high overhead, but its rays streaming down through the great window painted a brilliant band of light on the floor underfoot. Cutting across that band at an angle was another, much fainter one, so that the frame of the window threw a double shadow.

Poole had to go almost down on his knees so that he could peer up at the sky. He had thought himself beyond surprise, but the spectacle of two suns left him momentarily speechless.

"What's that?" he gasped, when he had recovered his breath.

"Oh—haven't you been told? That's Lucifer."

"Earth has another sun?"

"Well, it doesn't give us much heat, but it's put the Moon out of business . . . Before the Second Mission went there to look for you, that was the planet Jupiter."

I knew I would have much to learn in this new world, Poole told himself. But just how much, I never dreamed.

5. EDUCATION

Poole was both astonished and delighted when the television set was wheeled into the room and positioned at the end of his bed. Delighted, because he was suffering from mild information starvation—and astonished because it was a model that had been obsolete even in his own time.

"We've had to promise the Museum we'll give it back," Matron informed him. "And I expect you know how to use this."

As he fondled the remote control, Poole felt a wave of acute nostalgia sweep over him. As few other artifacts could, it brought back memories of his childhood, and the days when most television sets were too stupid to understand spoken commands.

"Thank you, Matron. What's the best news channel?"

She seemed puzzled by his question, then brightened.

"Oh—I see what you mean. But Professor Anderson thinks you're not quite ready yet. So Archives has put together a collection that will make you feel at home."

Poole wondered briefly what the storage medium was in this day and age. He could still remember compact discs, and his eccentric old Uncle George had been the proud possessor of a vintage LP collection. But surely that technological contest must have finished centuries ago—in the usual Darwinian way, with the survival of the fittest.

He had to admit that the selection was well done, by someone (Indra?) familiar with the early Twenty-first Century. There was nothing disturbing—no wars or violence, and very little contemporary business or politics, all of which would now be utterly irrelevant. There were some light comedies, sporting events (how did they know that he had been a keen tennis fan?), classical and pop music, and wildlife documentaries.

And whoever had put this collection together must have had a sense of humor, or they would not have included episodes from each *Star Trek* series. As a very small boy, Poole had met both Patrick Stewart and Leonard Nimoy: he wondered what they would have thought, could they have known the destiny of the child who had shyly asked for their autographs.

A depressing thought occurred to him, soon after he had started exploring—much of the time in Fast Forward—these relics of the past. He had read somewhere that by the turn of the century—his century!—there were approximately fifty thousand television stations broadcasting simultaneously. If that figure had been maintained—and it might well have increased—by now millions of millions of hours of TV programming must have gone on the air. So even the most hardened cynic would admit that there were probably at least a billion hours of worthwhile viewing . . . and millions that would pass the highest standards of excellence. How to find these few needles in so gigantic a haystack?

The thought was so overwhelming—indeed, so demoralizing—that after a week of increasingly aimless channel-surfing Poole asked for the set to be removed. Perhaps fortunately, he had less and less time to himself during his waking hours, which were steadily growing longer as his strength came back.

There was no risk of boredom, thanks to the continual parade not only of serious researchers but also inquisitive—and presumably influential—citizens who had managed to filter past the palace guard established by Matron and Professor Anderson. Nevertheless, he was glad when, one day, the television set reappeared; he was beginning to suffer withdrawal symptoms—and this time, he resolved to be more selective in his viewing.

The venerable antique was accompanied by Indra Wallace, smiling broadly.

"We've found something you must see, Frank. We think it will help you to adjust—anyway, we're sure you'll enjoy it."

Poole had always found that remark a recipe for guaranteed boredom, and prepared for the worst. But the opening had him instantly hooked, taking him back to his old life as few other things could have done. At once he recognized one of the most famous voices of his age, and remembered that he had seen this very program before.

"Atlanta, December 31, 2000 . . .

"This is CNN International, five minutes from the dawn of the New Millennium, with all its unknown perils and promise . . .

"But before we try to explore the future, let's look back a thousand years, and ask ourselves: 'Could any persons living in A.D. 1000 even remotely imagine our world, or understand it, if they were magically transported across the centuries?'

"Almost the whole of the technology we take for granted was invented near the very end of our Millennium—most of it in the last two hundred years. The steam engine, electricity, telephones, radio, television, cinema, aviation, electronics—and, during a single lifetime, nuclear energy and space travel—what would the greatest minds of the past have made of these? How long could an Archimedes or a Leonardo have retained his sanity, if suddenly dumped into our world?

"It's tempting to think that we would do better, if we were transported a thousand years hence. Surely the fundamental scientific discoveries have already been made: though there will be major improvements in technology, will there be any devices, anything as magical and incomprehensible to us as a pocket calculator or a video camera would have been to Isaac Newton?

"Perhaps our age is indeed sundered from all those that have gone before. Telecommunications, the ability to record images and sounds once irrevocably lost, the conquest of the air and space—all these have created a civilization beyond the wildest fantasies of the past. And equally important, Copernicus, Newton, Darwin, and Einstein have so changed our modes of thinking and our outlook on the universe that we might seem almost a new species to the most brilliant of our predecessors.

"And will our successors, a thousand years from now, look back on us with the same pity with which we regard our ignorant, superstitious, disease-ridden, short-lived ancestors? We believe that we know the answers to questions that they could not even ask: but what surprises does the Third Millennium hold for us?

"Well, here it comes—"

A great bell began to toll the strokes of midnight. The last vibration throbbed into silence . . .

"And that's the way it was—goodbye, wonderful and terrible Twentieth Century . . ."

Then the picture broke into a myriad of fragments, and a new commentator took over, speaking with the accent Poole could now easily understand that immediately brought him up to the present.

"Now, in the first minutes of the year 3001, we can answer that question from the past . . .

"Certainly, the people of 2001 who you were just watching would not feel as utterly overwhelmed in our age as someone from 1001 would have been in theirs. Many of our technological achievements they would have anticipated; indeed they would have expected satellite cities, and colonies on the Moon and planets. They might even have been disappointed, because we are not yet immortal, and have sent probes only to the nearest stars . . ."

Abruptly, Indra switched off the recording.

"See the rest later, Frank; you're getting tired. But I hope it will help you to adjust."

"Thank you, Indra. I'll have to sleep on it. But it's certainly proved one point."

"What's that?"

"I should be grateful I'm not a thousand-and-oner, dropped into 2001. That would be too much of a quantum jump: I don't believe anyone could adjust to it. At least I know about electricity, and won't die of fright if a picture starts talking at me."

I hope, Poole told himself, that confidence is justified. Someone once said that any sufficiently advanced technology is indistinguishable from magic. Will I meet magic in this new world—and be able to handle it?

6. BRAINCAP

"I'm afraid you'll have to make an agonizing decision," said Professor Anderson, with a smile that neutralized the exaggerated gravity of his words.

"I can take it, Doctor. Just give it to me straight."

"Before you can be fitted with your Braincap, you have to be completely bald. So here's your choice. At the rate your hair grows, you'd have to be shaved at least once a month. Or you could have a permanent."

"How's that done?"

"Laser scalp treatment. Kills the follicles at the roots."

"Hmm . . . is it reversible?"

"Yes, but that's messy and painful, and takes weeks."

"Then I'll see how I like being hairless, before committing myself. I can't forget what happened to Samson."

"Who?"

"Character in a famous old book. His girlfriend cut off his hair while he was sleeping. When he woke up, all his strength had gone."

"Now I remember—pretty obvious medical symbolism!"

"Still, I wouldn't mind losing my beard—I'd be happy to stop shaving, once and for all."

"I'll make the arrangements. And what kind of wig would you like?"

Poole laughed.

"I'm not particularly vain—think it would be a nuisance, and probably won't bother. Something else I can decide later."

That everyone in this era was artificially bald was a surprising fact that Poole had been quite slow to discover; his first revelation had come when both of his nurses removed their luxuriant tresses, without the slightest sign of embarrassment, just before several equally bald specialists arrived to give him a series of microbiological checks. He had never been surrounded by so many hairless people, and his initial guess was that this was the latest step in the medical profession's endless war against germs.

Like many of his guesses, it was completely wrong, and when he discovered the true reason he amused himself by seeing how often he would have been sure, had he not known in advance, that his visitors' hair was not their own. The answer was "Seldom with men: never with women"; this was obviously the great age of the wig-maker.

Professor Anderson wasted no time: that afternoon the nurses smeared some evil-smelling cream over Poole's head, and when he looked into the mirror an hour later he did not recognize himself. Well, he thought, perhaps a wig would be a good idea, after all . . .

The Braincap fitting took somewhat longer. First a mold had to be made, which required him to sit motionless for a few minutes until the plaster set. He fully expected to be told that his head was the wrong shape, when his nurses—giggling most unprofessionally—had a hard time extricating him. "Ouch—that hurt!" he complained.

Next came the skullcap itself, a metal helmet that fitted snugly almost down to the ears, and triggered a nostalgic thought—"Wish my Jewish friends could see me now!" After a few minutes, it was so comfortable that he was unaware of its presence.

Now he was ready for the installation—a process which, he now realized with something akin to awe, had been the Rite of Passage for almost all the human race for more than half a millennium.

"There's no need to close your eyes," said the technician, who had been introduced by the pretentious title of "Brain Engineer"—almost always shortened to "Brainman" in popular usage. "When Setup begins, all your inputs will be taken over. Even if your eyes are open, you won't see anything."

I wonder if everyone feels as nervous as this, Poole asked himself. Is this the last moment I'll be in control of my own mind? Still, I've learned to trust the technology of this age; up to now, it hasn't let me down. Of course, as the old saying goes, there's always a first time . . .

As he had been promised, he had felt nothing except a gentle tickling as the myriads of nanowires wormed their way through his scalp. All his senses were still perfectly normal; when he scanned his familiar room, everything was exactly where it should be.

The Brainman—wearing his own skullcap, wired, like Poole's, to a piece of equipment that could easily have been mistaken for a Twentieth-Century laptop computer—gave him a reassuring smile.

"Ready?" he asked.

There were times when the old clichés were the best ones.

"Ready as I'll ever be," Poole answered.

Slowly, the light faded—or seemed to. A great silence descended, and even the gentle gravity of the Tower relinquished its hold upon him. He was an embryo, floating in a featureless void, though not in complete darkness. He had known such a barely visible, near ultraviolet tenebrosity, on the very edge of night, only once in his life—when he had descended farther than was altogether wise, down the face of a sheer cliff at the outer edge of the Great Barrier Reef. Looking down into hundreds of meters of crystalline emptiness, he had felt such a sense of disorientation that he experienced a brief moment of panic, and had almost triggered his buoyancy unit before regaining control. Needless to say, he had never mentioned the incident to the Space Agency physicians . . .

From a great distance, a voice spoke out of the immense void that now seemed to surround him. But it did not reach him through his ears: it sounded softly in the echoing labyrinths of his brain.

"Calibration starting. From time to time you will be asked questions—you can answer mentally, but it may help to vocalize. Do you understand?"

"Yes," Poole replied, wondering if his lips were indeed moving. There was no way that he could tell.

Something was appearing in the void—a grid of thin lines, like a huge sheet of graph paper. It extended up and down, right and left, to the limits of his vision. He tried to move his head, but the image refused to change.

Numbers started to flicker across the grid, too fast for him to read—but presumably some circuit was recording them. Poole could not help smiling (did his cheeks move?) at the familiarity of it all. This was just like the computer-driven eye examination that any oculist of his age would give a client.

The grid vanished, to be replaced by smooth sheets of color filling his entire field of view. In a few seconds, they flashed from one end of the spectrum to the other. "Could have told you that," Poole muttered silently. "My color vision's perfect. Next for hearing, I suppose."

He was quite correct. A faint, drumming sound accelerated until it became the lowest of audible C's, then raced up the musical scale until it disappeared beyond the auditory range of human beings, into bat and dolphin territory.

That was the last of the simple, straightforward tests. He was briefly assailed by scents and flavors, most of them pleasant but some quite the reverse. Then he became, or so it seemed, a puppet on an invisible string.

He presumed that his neuromuscular control was being tested, and hoped that there were no external manifestations; if there were, he would probably look like someone in the terminal stages of St. Vitus' dance. And for one moment he even had a violent erection, but was unable to give it a reality check before he fell into a dreamless sleep.

Or did he only dream that he slept? He had no idea how much time had elapsed before he awoke. The helmet had already gone, together with the Brainman and his equipment.

"Everything went fine," beamed Matron. "It will take a few hours to check that there are no anomalies. If your reading's K.O.—I mean O.K.—you'll have your Braincap tomorrow."

Poole appreciated the efforts of his entourage to learn archaic English, but he could not help wishing that Matron had not made that unfortunate slip of the tongue.

When the time came for the final fitting, Poole felt almost like a boy again, about to unwrap some wonderful new toy under the Christmas tree.

"You won't have to go through all that setting-up again," the Brainman assured him. "Download will start immediately. I'll give you a five-minute demo. Just relax and enjoy."

Gentle, soothing music washed over him; though it was something very familiar, from his own time, he could not identify it. There was a mist before his eyes, which parted as he walked toward it . . .

Yes, he was walking! The illusion was utterly convincing; he could feel the impact of his feet on the ground, and now that the music had stopped he could hear a gentle wind blowing through the great trees that appeared to surround him. He recognized them as California redwoods, and hoped that they still existed in reality, somewhere on Earth.

He was moving at a brisk pace—too fast for comfort, as if time was slightly accelerated so he could cover as much ground as possible. Yet he was not conscious of any effort; he felt he was a guest in someone else's body. The sensation was enhanced by the fact that he had no control over his movements. When he attempted to stop, or to change direction, nothing happened. He was going along for the ride.

It did not matter; he was enjoying the novel experience—and could appreciate how addictive it could become. The "dream machines" that many scientists of his own century had anticipated—often with alarm—were now part of everyday life. Poole wondered how mankind had managed to survive: he had been told that much of it had not. Millions had been brain-burned, and had dropped out of life.

Of course, he would be immune to such temptations! He would use this marvelous tool to learn more about the world of the Third Millennium, and to acquire in minutes new skills that would otherwise take years to master. Well—he might, just occasionally, use the Braincap purely for fun . . .

He had come to the edge of the forest, and was looking out across a wide river. Without hesitation, he walked into it, and felt no alarm as the water rose over his head. It did seem a little strange that he could continue breathing naturally, but he thought it much more remarkable that he could see perfectly in a medium where the unaided human eye could not focus. He could count every scale on the magnificent trout that went swimming past, apparently oblivious to this strange intruder.

A mermaid! Well, he had always wanted to meet one, but he had assumed that they were marine creatures. Perhaps they occasionally came upstream—like salmon, to have their babies? She was gone before he could question her, to confirm or deny this revolutionary theory.

The river ended in a translucent wall; he stepped through it onto the face of a desert, beneath a blazing sun. Its heat burned him uncomfortably—yet he was able to look directly into its noonday fury. He could even see, with unnatural clarity, an archipelago of sunspots near one limb. And—this was surely impossible!—there was the tenuous glory of the corona, quite invisible except during total eclipse, reaching out like a swan's wings on either side of the sun.

Everything faded to black: the haunting music returned, and with it the blissful coolness of his familiar room. He opened his eyes (had they ever been closed?) and found an expectant audience waiting for his reaction.

"Wonderful!" he breathed, almost reverently. "Some of it seemed—well, realer than real!"

Then his engineer's curiosity, never far from the surface, started nagging him.

"Even that short demo must have contained an enormous amount of information. How's it stored?"

"In these tablets—the same ones your audiovisual system uses, but with much greater capacity."

The Brainman handed Poole a small square, apparently made of glass, silvered on one surface; it was almost the same size as the computer diskettes of his youth, but twice the thickness. As Poole tilted it back and forth, trying to see into its transparent interior, there were occasional rainbow-hued flashes, but that was all.

He was holding, he realized, the end product of more than a thousand years of electro-optical technology—as well as other technologies unborn in his era. And it was not surprising that, superficially, it closely resembled the devices he had known. There was a convenient shape and size for most of the common objects of everyday life— knives and forks, books, hand tools, furniture—and removable memories for computers.

"What's its capacity?" he asked. "In my time, we were up to a terabyte in something this size. I'm sure you've done a lot better."

"Not as much as you might imagine—there's a limit, of course, set by the structure of matter. By the way, what was a terabyte? Afraid I've forgotten."

"Shame on you! Kilo, mega, giga, tera . . . that's ten to the twelfth bytes. Then the petabyte—ten to the fifteenth—that's as far as I ever got."

"That's about where we start. It's enough to record everything any person can experience during one lifetime."

It was an astonishing thought, yet it should not have been so surprising. The kilogram of jelly inside the human skull was not much larger than the tablet Poole was holding in his hand, and it could not possibly be as efficient a storage device—it had so many other duties to deal with.

"And that's not all," the Brainman continued. "With some data compression, it could store not only the memories—but the actual person."

"And reproduce them again?"

"Of course; straightforward job of nanoassembly."

So I'd heard, Poole told himself, but I never really believed it.

Back in his century, it seemed wonderful enough that the entire lifework of a great artist could be stored on a single small disk.

And now, something no larger could hold—the artist as well.

7. DEBRIEFING

"I'm delighted," said Poole, "to know that the Smithsonian still exists, after all these centuries."

"You probably wouldn't recognize it," said the visitor who had introduced himself as Dr. Alistair Kim, Director of Astronautics. "Especially as it's now scattered over the Solar System—the main off-Earth collections are on Mars and the Moon, and many of the exhibits that legally belong to us are still heading for the stars. Someday we'll catch up with them and bring them home. We're particularly anxious to get our hands on *Pioneer 10*—the first man-made object to escape from the Solar System."

"I believe I was on the verge of doing that, when they located me."

"Lucky for you—and for us. You may be able to throw light on many things we don't know."

"Frankly, I doubt it—but I'll do my best. I don't remember a thing after that runaway space-pod charged me. Though I still find it hard to believe, I've been told that Hal was responsible."

"That's true, but it's a complicated story. Everything we've been able to learn is in this recording—about twenty hours, but you can probably Fast most of it.

"You know, of course, that Dave Bowman went out in the Number 2 Pod to rescue you—but was then locked outside the ship because Hal refused to open the pod-bay doors."

"Why, for God's sake?"

Dr. Kim winced slightly. It was not the first time Poole had noticed such a reaction.

(Must watch my language, he thought. "God" seems to be a dirty word in this culture—must ask Indra about it.)

"There was a major programming error in Hal's instructions—he'd been given control of aspects of the mission you and Bowman didn't know about. It's all in the recording . . .

"Anyway, he also cut off the life-support systems to the three hybernauts—the Alpha Crew—and Bowman had to jettison their bodies as well."

(So Dave and I were the Beta Crew—something else I didn't know . . .)

"What happened to them?" Poole asked. "Couldn't they have been rescued, just as I was?"

"I'm afraid not: we've looked into it, of course. Bowman ejected them several hours after he'd taken back control from Hal, so their orbits were slightly different from yours. Just enough for them to burn up in Jupiter—while you skimmed by, and got a gravity boost that would have taken you to the Orion Nebula in a few thousand more years . . .

"Doing everything on manual override—really a fantastic performance!—Bowman managed to get *Discovery* into orbit round Jupiter. And there he encountered what the Second Expedition called Big Brother—an apparent twin of the Tycho Monolith, but hundreds of times larger.

"And that's where we lost him. He left *Discovery* in the remaining space-pod, and made a rendezvous with Big Brother. For almost a thousand years, we've been haunted by his last message: 'By Deus—it's full of stars!' "

(Here we go again! Poole told himself. No way Dave could have said that . . . Must have been "My God—it's full of stars!")

"Apparently the pod was drawn into the Monolith by some kind of inertial field, because it—and presumably Bowman—survived an acceleration that should have crushed them instantly. And that was the last information anyone had, for almost ten years, until the joint U.S.–Russian *Leonov* mission."

"Which made a rendezvous with the abandoned *Discovery* so that Dr. Chandra could go aboard and reactivate Hal. Yes, I know that."

Dr. Kim looked slightly embarrassed.

"Sorry—I wasn't sure how much you'd been told already. Anyway, that's when even stranger things started to happen.

"Apparently the arrival of *Leonov* triggered something inside Big

Brother. If we did not have these recordings, no one would have believed what happened. Let me show you . . . here's Dr. Heywood Floyd keeping the midnight watch aboard *Discovery*, after power had been restored. Of course you'll recognize everything."

(Indeed I do: and how strange to see the long-dead Heywood Floyd, sitting in my old seat with Hal's unblinking red eye surveying everything in sight. And even stranger to think that Hal and I have both shared the same experience of resurrection from the dead . . .)

A message was coming up on one of the monitors, and Floyd answered lazily, "Okay, Hal. Who is calling?"

NO IDENTIFICATION.

Floyd looked slightly annoyed.

"Very well. Please give me the message."

IT IS DANGEROUS TO REMAIN HERE. YOU MUST LEAVE WITHIN FIFTEEN DAYS.

"That is absolutely impossible. Our launch window does not open until twenty-six days from now. We do not have sufficient propellant for an earlier departure."

I AM AWARE OF THESE FACTS. NEVERTHELESS YOU MUST LEAVE WITHIN FIFTEEN DAYS.

"I cannot take this warning seriously unless I know its origin . . . who is speaking to me?"

I WAS DAVID BOWMAN. IT IS IMPORTANT THAT YOU BELIEVE ME. LOOK BEHIND YOU.

Heywood Floyd slowly turned in his swivel chair, away from the banked panels and switches of the computer display, toward the Velcro-covered catwalk behind.

("Watch this carefully," said Dr. Kim.

As if I needed telling, thought Poole . . .)

The zero-gravity environment of *Discovery*'s observation deck was much dustier than he remembered it: he guessed that the air-filtration plant had not yet been brought on-line. The parallel rays of the distant yet still brilliant sun, streaming through the great windows, lit up myriads of dancing motes in a classic display of Brownian movement.

And now something strange was happening to these particles of dust; some force seemed to be marshaling them, herding them away from a central point yet bringing others toward it, until they all met on the surface of a hollow sphere. That sphere, about a meter across, hovered in the air for a moment like a giant soap bubble. Then it elongated into an ellipsoid, whose surface began to pucker, to form

folds and indentations. Poole was not really surprised when it started
to assume the shape of a man.

He had seen such figures, blown out of glass, in museums and science exhibitions. But this dusty phantom did not even approximate
anatomical accuracy; it was like a crude clay figurine, or one of the
primitive works of art found in the recesses of Stone Age caves. Only
the head was fashioned with care; and the face, beyond all shadow of
doubt, was that of Commander David Bowman.

HELLO, DR. FLOYD. NOW DO YOU BELIEVE ME.

The lips of the figure never moved: Poole realized that the voice—
yes, certainly Bowman's voice—was actually coming from the speaker
grille.

THIS IS VERY DIFFICULT FOR ME, AND I HAVE LITTLE TIME. I HAVE
BEEN ALLOWED TO GIVE THIS WARNING. YOU HAVE ONLY FIFTEEN DAYS.

"Why—and what are you?"

But the ghostly figure was already fading, its grainy envelope beginning to dissolve back into the constituent particles of dust.

GOODBYE, DR. FLOYD. WE CAN HAVE NO FURTHER CONTACT. BUT
THERE MAY BE ONE MORE MESSAGE, IF ALL GOES WELL.

As the image dissolved, Poole could not help smiling at that old
Space Age cliché. "If all goes well"—how many times he had heard
that phrase intoned before a mission!

The phantom vanished: only the motes of dancing dust were left,
resuming their random patterns in the air. With an effort of will, Poole
came back to the present.

"Well, Commander—what do you think of that?" asked Kim.

Poole was still shaken, and it was several seconds before he could
reply.

"The face and the voice were Bowman's—I'd swear to that. But
what was it?"

"That's what we're still arguing about. Call it a hologram, a projection—of course, there are plenty of ways it could be faked if anyone
wanted to—but not in those circumstances! And then, of course,
there's what happened next."

"Lucifer?"

"Yes. Thanks to that warning, they had just sufficient time to get
away, before Jupiter detonated."

"So whatever it was, the Bowman-thing was friendly and trying to
help."

"Presumably. And that's not the last time it appeared. It may have been responsible for that 'one more message,' warning us not to attempt any landings on Europa."

"And we never have?"

"Only once, by accident—when *Galaxy* was hijacked and forced down there, thirty-six years later, and her sister-ship *Universe* had to go to the rescue. It's all here—with what little our robot monitors have told us about the Europans."

"I'm anxious to see them."

"They're amphibious, and come in all shapes and sizes. As soon as Lucifer started melting the ice that covered their whole world, they began to emerge from the sea. Since then, they've developed at a speed that seems biologically impossible."

"From what I remember about Europa, weren't there lots of cracks in the ice? Perhaps they'd already started crawling through and having a look round."

"That's a widely accepted theory. But there's another, much more speculative, one. The Monolith may have been involved, in ways we don't yet understand. What triggered that line of thought was the discovery of TMA-0, right here on Earth, almost five hundred years after your time. I suppose you've been told about that?"

"Only vaguely—there's been so much to catch up with! I did think the name was ridiculous—since it wasn't a magnetic anomaly—and it was in Africa, not Tycho!"

"You're quite right, of course, but we're stuck with the name. And the more we learn about the Monoliths, the more the puzzle deepens. Especially as they're still the only real evidence for advanced technology beyond the Earth."

"That's surprised me. I should have thought that by this time we'd have picked up radio signals from somewhere. The astronomers started searching when I was a boy!"

"Well, there is one hint—and it's so terrifying that we don't like to talk about it. Have you heard of Nova Scorpio?"

"I don't believe so."

"Stars go nova all the time, of course—and this wasn't a particularly impressive one. But before it blew up, N Scorp was known to have several planets."

"Inhabited?"

"Absolutely no way of telling; radio searches had picked up nothing. And here's the nightmare . . .

"Luckily, the automatic Nova Patrol caught the event at the very beginning. And it didn't start at the star. One of the planets detonated first, and then triggered its sun."

"My Gah . . . sorry, go on."

"You see the point. It's impossible for a planet to go nova—except in one way."

"I once read a sick joke in a science-fiction novel—'Supernovae are industrial accidents.' "

"It wasn't a supernova—but that may be no joke. The most widely accepted theory is that someone else had been tapping vacuum energy—and had lost control."

"Or it could have been a war."

"Just as bad; we'll probably never know. But as our own civilization depends on the same energy source, you can understand why N Scorp sometimes gives us nightmares."

"And we only had melting nuclear reactors to worry about!"

"Not any longer, thank Deus. But I really wanted to tell you more about TMA-0's discovery, because it marked a turning point in human history.

"Finding TMA-1 on the Moon was a big enough shock, but five hundred years later there was a worse one. And it was much nearer home—in every sense of the word. Down there in Africa."

8. RETURN TO OLDUVAI

The Leakeys, Dr. Stephen Del Marco often told himself, would never have recognized this place, even though it's barely a dozen kilometers from where Louis and Mary, five centuries ago, dug up our first ancestors. Global warming, and the Little Ice Age (truncated by miracles of heroic technology) had transformed the landscape, and completely altered its biota. Oaks and pine trees were still fighting it out, to see which would survive the changes in climatic fortune.

And it was hard to believe that, by this year 2513, there was anything left in Olduvai undug by enthusiastic anthropologists. However, recent flash floods—which were not supposed to happen anymore— had resculpted this area, and cut away several meters of topsoil. Del Marco had taken advantage of the opportunity: and there, at the limit of the deep-scan, was something he could not quite believe.

It had taken more than a year of slow and careful excavation to reach that ghostly image, and to learn that the reality was stranger than anything he had dared to imagine. Robot digging machines had swiftly removed the first few meters, then the traditional slave-crews of graduate students had taken over. They had been helped—or hindered—by a team of four kongs, whom Del Marco considered more trouble than they were worth. However, the students adored the genetically enhanced gorillas, whom they treated like retarded but much-loved children. It was rumored that the relationships were not always completely platonic.

For the last few meters, however, everything was the work of human hands, usually wielding toothbrushes—soft-bristled at that. And now it was finished: Howard Carter, seeing the first glint of gold in Tutankhamen's tomb, had never uncovered such a treasure as this. From this moment onward, Del Marco knew, human beliefs and philosophies would be irrevocably changed.

The Monolith appeared to be the exact twin of that discovered on the Moon five centuries earlier: even the excavation surrounding it was almost identical in size. And like TMA-1, it was totally nonreflective, absorbing the fierce glare of the African sun and the pale gleam of Lucifer with equal indifference.

As he led his colleagues—the directors of the world's half-dozen most famous museums, three eminent anthropologists, the heads of two media empires—down into the pit, Del Marco wondered if such a distinguished group of men and women had ever been so silent, for so long. But that was the effect that this ebon rectangle had on all visitors, as they realized the implications of the thousands of artifacts that surrounded it.

For here was an archaeologist's treasure trove—crudely fashioned flint tools, countless bones—some animal, some human—and almost all arranged in careful patterns. For centuries—no, millennia—these pitiful gifts had been brought here, by creatures with only the first glimmer of intelligence, as tribute to a marvel beyond their understanding.

And beyond ours, Del Marco had often thought. Yet of two things he was certain, though he doubted if proof would ever be possible.

This was where—in time and space—the human species had really begun.

And this Monolith was the very first of all its multitudinous gods.

9. SKYLAND

"There were mice in my bedroom last night," Poole complained, only half seriously. "Is there any chance you could find me a cat?"

Dr. Wallace looked puzzled, then started to laugh.

"You must have heard one of the cleaning microts—I'll get the programming checked so they don't disturb you. Try not to step on one if you catch it at work; if you do, it will call for help, and all its friends will come to pick up the pieces."

So much to learn—so little time! No, that wasn't true, Poole reminded himself. He might well have a century ahead of him, thanks to the medical science of this age. The thought was already beginning to fill him with apprehension rather than pleasure.

At least he was now able to follow most conversations easily, and had learned to pronounce words so that Indra was not the only person who could understand him. He was very glad that Anglish was now the world language, though French, Russian, and Mandarin still flourished.

"I've another problem, Indra—and I guess you're the only person who can help. When I say 'God,' why do people look embarrassed?"

Indra did not look at all embarrassed; in fact, she laughed.

"That's a very complicated story. I wish my old friend Dr. Khan were here to explain it to you—but he's on Ganymede, curing any remaining True Believers he can find there. When all the old religions were discredited—let me tell you about Pope Pius XX sometime—one of the greatest men in history!—we still needed a word for the Prime Cause, or the Creator of the Universe—if there is one . . .

"There were lots of suggestions—Deo—Theo—Jove—Brahma—they were all tried, and some of them are still around—especially Einstein's favorite, 'The Old One.' But Deus seems to be the fashion nowadays."

"I'll try to remember; but it still seems silly to me."

"You'll get used to it: I'll teach you some other reasonably polite expletives, to use when you want to express your feelings . . ."

"You said that all the old religions have been discredited. So what do people believe nowadays?"

"As little as possible. We're all either Deists or Theists."

"You've lost me. Definitions, please."

"They were slightly different in your time, but here are the latest versions. Theists believe there's not more than one God; Deists that there is not less than one God."

"I'm afraid the distinction's too subtle for me."

"Not for everyone; you'd be amazed at the bitter controversies it's aroused. Five centuries ago, someone used what's known as surreal mathematics to prove there's an infinite number of grades between Theists and Deists. Of course, like most dabblers with infinity, he went insane. By the way, the best-known Deists were Americans—Washington, Franklin, Jefferson."

"A little before my time—though you'd be surprised how many people don't realize it."

"Now I've some good news. Joe—Proff Anderson—has finally given his—what was the phrase?—O.K. You're fit enough to be moved into permanent quarters."

"That *is* good news. Everyone here has treated me very well, but I'll be glad to have a place of my own."

"You'll need new clothes, and someone to show you how to wear them. And to help you with the hundreds of little everyday jobs that can waste so much time. So we've taken the liberty of arranging a personal assistant for you. Come in, Danil . . ."

Danil was a small, light-brown man in his mid-thirties, who surprised Poole by not giving him the usual palm-to-palm salute, with its automatic exchange of information. Indeed, it soon appeared that Danil did not possess an Ident: whenever it was needed, he produced a small rectangle of plastic that apparently served the same purpose as the Twenty-first-Century's "smart cards."

"Danil will also be your guide and—what was that word? I can never remember—rhymes with 'ballet.' He's been specially trained for the job. I'm sure you'll find him completely satisfactory."

Though Poole appreciated this gesture, it made him feel a little uncomfortable. A valet, indeed! He could not recall ever meeting one; in his time, they were already a rare and endangered species. He began to feel like a character from an early Twentieth-Century English novel.

"And while Danil is organizing your move, we'll go for a little trip upstairs . . . to the Lunar Level."

"Wonderful. How far is that?"

"Oh, about twelve thousand kilometers."

"Twelve thousand! That will take hours!"

Indra looked surprised at his remark, then she smiled.

"Not as long as you think. No—we don't have a *Star Trek* Transporter yet—though I believe they're still working on it! So you have a choice—though I know which one you'll take. We can go up on an external elevator, and admire the view—or an interior one, and enjoy a meal and some light entertainment."

"I can't imagine anyone wanting to stay inside."

"You'd be surprised. It's too vertiginous for some people—especially visitors from down below. Even mountain climbers who say they've got a head for heights may start to turn green when the heights are measured in thousands of kilometers, instead of meters."

"I'll risk it," Poole answered with a smile. "I've been higher."

When they had passed through a double set of airlocks in the exterior wall of the Tower (was it imagination, or did he feel a curious sense of disorientation then?) they entered what might have been the auditorium of a very small theater. Rows of ten seats were banked up in five tiers: they all faced toward one of the huge picture windows that Poole still found disconcerting, as he could never quite forget the hundreds of tons of air pressure striving to blast it out into space.

The dozen or so other passengers, who had probably never given the matter any thought, seemed perfectly at ease. They all smiled as they recognized him, nodded politely, then turned away to admire the view.

"Welcome to Skylounge," said the inevitable autovoice. "Ascent begins in five minutes. You will find refreshments and toilets on the lower floor."

Just how long will this trip last? Poole wondered. We're going to travel over twenty thousand klicks, there and back: this will be like no elevator ride I've ever known on Earth . . .

While he was waiting for the ascent to begin, he enjoyed the stunning panorama laid out two thousand kilometers below. It was winter in the Northern Hemisphere, but the climate had indeed changed drastically, for there was little snow south of the Arctic Circle.

Europe was almost cloud-free, and there was so much detail that the eye was overwhelmed. One by one he identified the great cities whose names had echoed down the centuries; they had been shrinking even in his time, as the communications revolution changed the face of the world, and had now dwindled still further. There were also some bodies of water in improbable places—the northern Sahara's Lake Saladin was almost a small sea.

Poole was so engrossed by the view that he had forgotten the passage of time. Suddenly he realized that much more than five minutes had passed—yet the elevator was still stationary. Had something gone wrong, or were they waiting for late arrivals?

And then he noticed something so extraordinary that at first he refused to believe the evidence of his eyes. The panorama had expanded, as if he had already risen hundreds of kilometers! Even as he watched, he noticed new features of the planet below creeping into the frame of the window.

Then Poole laughed, as the obvious explanation occurred to him.

"You could have fooled me, Indra! I thought this was real—not a video projection!"

Indra looked back at him with a quizzical smile.

"Think again, Frank. We started to move about ten minutes ago. By now we must be climbing at, oh, at least a thousand kilometers an hour. Though I'm told these elevators can reach a hundred gee at maximum acceleration, we won't touch more than ten, on this short run."

"That's impossible! Six is the maximum they ever gave me in the centrifuge, and I didn't enjoy weighing half a ton. I know we haven't moved since we stepped inside."

Poole had raised his voice slightly, and suddenly became aware that the other passengers were pretending not to notice.

"I don't understand how it's done, Frank, but it's called an inertial field. Or sometimes a Sharp one—the 'S' stands for a famous Russian scientist, Sakharov—I don't know who the others were."

Slowly, understanding dawned in Poole's mind—and also a sense of awestruck wonder. Here indeed was a "technology indistinguishable from magic."

"Some of my friends used to dream of 'space drives'—energy fields that could replace rockets, and allow movement without any feeling of acceleration. Most of us thought they were crazy, but it seems they were right! I can still hardly believe it . . . and unless I'm mistaken, we're starting to lose weight."

"Yes—it's adjusting to the lunar value. When we step out, you'll feel we're on the Moon. But for goodness sake, Frank—forget you're an engineer, and simply enjoy the view."

It was good advice, but even as he watched the whole of Africa, Europe, and much of Asia flow into his field of vision, Poole could not tear his mind away from this astonishing revelation. Yet he should not have been wholly surprised: he knew that there had been major breakthroughs in space propulsion systems since his time, but had not realized that they would have such dramatic applications to everyday life—if that term could be applied to existence in a thirty-six-thousand-kilometer-high skyscraper.

And the age of the rocket must have been over centuries ago. All his knowledge of propellant systems and combustion chambers, ion thrusters and fusion reactors, was totally obsolete. Of course, that no longer mattered—but he understood the sadness that the skipper of a windjammer must have felt, when sail gave way to steam.

His mood changed abruptly, and he could not help smiling, when the autovoice announced "Arriving in two minutes. Please make sure that you do not leave any of your personal belongings behind."

How often he had heard that announcement, on some commercial flight! He looked at his watch, and was surprised to see that they had been ascending for less than half an hour. So that meant an average speed of at least twenty thousand kilometers an hour, yet they might never have moved. What was even stranger—for the last ten minutes or more they must actually have been decelerating so rapidly that by rights they should all have been standing on the roof, heads pointing toward Earth!

The doors opened silently, and as Poole stepped out he again felt the slight disorientation he had noticed on entering the elevator lounge. This time, however, he knew what it meant: he was moving through the transition zone where the inertial field overlapped with gravity—at this level, equal to the Moon's.

Though the view of the receding Earth had been awesome, even for an astronaut, there was nothing unexpected or surprising about it. But who would have imagined a gigantic chamber, apparently occupying the entire width of the Tower, so that the far wall was more than five kilometers away? Perhaps by this time there were larger enclosed volumes on the Moon and Mars, but this must surely be one of the largest in space itself.

They were standing on a viewing platform, fifty meters up on the outer wall, looking across an astonishingly varied panorama. Obviously, an attempt had been made to reproduce a whole range of terrestrial biomes. Immediately beneath them was a group of slender trees that Poole could not at first identify: then he realized that they were oaks, adapted to one sixth of their normal gravity. What, he wondered, would palm trees look like here? Giant reeds, probably . . .

In the middle distance there was a small lake, fed by a river that meandered across a grassy plain, then disappeared into something that looked like a single gigantic banyan tree. What was the source of the water? Poole had become aware of a faint drumming sound, and as he swept his gaze along the gently curving wall, he discovered a miniature Niagara, with a perfect rainbow hovering in the spray above it.

He could have stood there for hours, admiring the view and still not exhausting all the wonders of this complex and brilliantly contrived simulation of the planet below. As it spread out into new and hostile environments, perhaps the human race felt an ever-increasing need to remember its origins. Of course, even in his own time every city had its parks as—usually feeble—reminders of Nature. The same impulse must be acting here, on a much grander scale. Central Park, Africa Tower!

"Let's go down," said Indra. "There's so much to see, and I don't come here as often as I'd like."

Though walking was almost effortless in this low gravity, from time to time they took advantage of a small monorail, and stopped once for refreshments at a café, cunningly concealed in the trunk of a redwood that must have been at least a quarter of a kilometer tall.

There were very few other people about—their fellow-passengers had long since disappeared into the landscape—so it was as if they had all this wonderland to themselves. Everything was so beautifully maintained, presumably by armies of robots, that occasionally Poole was reminded of a visit he had made to Disney World as a small boy.

But this was even better: there were no crowds, and indeed very little reminder of the human race and its artifacts.

They were admiring a superb collection of orchids, some of enormous size, when Poole had one of the biggest shocks of his life. As they walked past a typical small gardener's shed, the door opened—and the gardener emerged.

Frank Poole had always prided himself on his self-control, and never imagined that as a full-grown adult he would give a cry of pure fright. But like every boy of his generation, he had seen all the *Jurassic* movies—and he knew a raptor, when he met one eye to eye.

"I'm terribly sorry," said Indra, with obvious concern. "I never thought of warning you."

Poole's jangling nerves returned to normal. Of course, there could be no danger, in this perhaps too-well-ordered world, but still . . . !

The dinosaur returned his stare with apparent total disinterest, then doubled back into the shed and emerged again with a rake and a pair of garden shears, which it dropped into a bag hanging over one shoulder. It walked away from them with a birdlike gait, never looking back as it disappeared behind some ten-meter-high sunflowers.

"I should explain," said Indra contritely. "We like to use bio-organisms when we can, rather than robots—I suppose it's carbon chauvinism! Now, there are only a few animals that have any manual dexterity, and we've used them all at one time or another.

"And here's a mystery that no one's been able to solve. You'd think that enhanced herbivores like chimps and gorillas would be good at this sort of work. Well, they're not; they don't have the patience for it.

"Yet carnivores like our friend here are excellent, and easily trained. What's more—here's another paradox!—after they've been modified, they're docile and good-natured. Of course, there's almost a thousand years of genetic engineering behind them, and look what primitive man did to the wolf, merely by trial and error!"

Indra laughed and continued: "You may not believe this, Frank, but they also make good baby-sitters—children love them! There's a five-hundred-year-old joke: 'Would you trust your kids to a dinosaur? What—and risk injuring it!' "

Poole joined in the laughter, partly in shame-faced reaction to his own fright. To change the subject, he asked Indra the question that was still worrying him.

"All this," he said, "it's wonderful—but why go to so much trouble, when anyone in the Tower can reach the real thing, just as quickly?"

Indra looked at him thoughtfully, weighing her words.

"That's not quite true. It's uncomfortable—even dangerous—for anyone who lives above the half-gee level to go down to Earth, even in a hoverchair."

"Not for me, surely! I was born and bred at one gee—and never neglected my exercises aboard *Discovery*."

"You'll have to take that up with Proff Anderson. Perhaps I shouldn't tell you this, but there's a big argument going on about the current setting of your biological clock. Apparently it never stopped completely, and guesses of your equivalent age range from fifty to seventy. Though you're doing fine, you can't expect to regain your full strength—after a thousand years!"

Now I begin to understand, Poole told himself bleakly. That explained Anderson's evasiveness, and all the muscular reaction tests he had been doing.

I've come all the way back from Jupiter, to within two thousand kilometers of Earth—but however often I visit it in virtual reality, I may never again walk on the surface of my home planet.

I'm not sure how I will be able to handle this . . .

10. HOMAGE TO ICARUS

His depression quickly passed: there was so much to do and see. A thousand lifetimes would not have been enough, and the problem was to choose which of the myriad distractions this age could offer. He tried, not always successfully, to avoid the trivia, and to concentrate on the things that mattered—notably his education.

The Braincap—and the book-sized player that went with it, inevitably called the Brainbox—was of enormous value here. He soon had a small library of "instant knowledge" tablets, each containing all the material needed for a college degree. When he slipped one of these into the Brainbox, and gave it the speed and intensity adjustments that most suited him, there would be a flash of light, followed by a period of unconsciousness that might last as long as an hour. When he awoke, it seemed that new areas of his mind had been opened up, though he only knew they were there when he searched for them. It was almost as if he was the owner of a library who had suddenly discovered shelves of books he did not know he had possessed.

To a large extent, he was the master of his own time. Out of a sense of duty—and gratitude—he acceded to as many requests as he could from scientists, historians, writers, and artists working in media that were often incomprehensible to him. He also had countless invitations from other citizens of the four Towers, virtually all of which he was compelled to turn down.

Most tempting—and most hard to resist—were those that came from the beautiful planet spread out below. "Of course," Professor Anderson had told him, "you'd survive if you went down for a short time with the right life-support system, but you wouldn't enjoy it. And it might weaken your neuromuscular system even further. It's never really recovered from that thousand-year sleep."

His other guardian, Indra Wallace, protected him from unnecessary intrusions, and advised him which requests he should accept—and which he should politely refuse. By himself, he would never understand the sociopolitical structure of this incredibly complex culture, but he soon gathered that, although in theory all class distinctions had vanished, there were a few thousand super-citizens. George Orwell had been right; some would always be more equal than others.

There had been times when, conditioned by his Twenty-first-Century experience, Poole had wondered who was paying for all this hospitality—would he one day be presented with the equivalent of an enormous hotel bill? But Indra had quickly reassured him: he was a unique and priceless museum exhibit, so would never have to worry about such mundane considerations. Anything he wanted—within reason—would be made available to him: Poole wondered what the limits were, never imagining that one day he would attempt to discover them.

All the most important things in life happen by accident, and he had set his wall display browser on random scan, silent, when a striking image caught his attention.

"Stop scan! Sound up!" he shouted, with quite unnecessary loudness.

He recognized the music, but it was a few minutes before he identified it; the fact that his wall was filled with winged humans circling gracefully round each other undoubtedly helped. But Tschaikovsky would have been utterly astonished to see this performance of *Swan Lake*—with the dancers actually flying . . .

Poole watched, entranced, for several minutes, until he was fairly confident that this was reality, and not a simulation: even in his own day, one could never be quite certain. Presumably the ballet was being performed in one of the many low-gravity environments—a very large one, judging by some of the images. It might even be here in Africa Tower.

I want to try that, Poole decided. He had never quite forgiven the Space Agency for banning one of his greatest pleasures, delayed parachute formation jumping, even though he could see the Agency's point in not wanting to risk a valuable investment. The doctors had been quite unhappy about his earlier hang-gliding accident; fortunately, his teenage bones had healed completely.

"Well," he thought, "there's no one to stop me now . . . unless it's Proff Anderson . . ."

To Poole's relief, the physician thought it an excellent idea, and he was also pleased to find that every one of the Towers had its own Aviary, up at the one-tenth gee level.

Within a few days he was being measured for his wings, not in the least like the elegant versions worn by the performers of *Swan Lake*. Instead of feathers there was a flexible membrane, and when he grasped the handholds attached to the supporting ribs, Poole realized that he must look much more like a bat than a bird. However, his "Move over, Dracula!" was completely wasted on his instructor, who was apparently unacquainted with vampires.

For his first lessons he was restrained by a light harness, so that he did not move anywhere while he was taught the basic strokes—and, most important of all, learned control and stability. Like many acquired skills, it was not quite as easy as it looked.

He felt ridiculous in this safety-harness—how could anyone injure themselves at a tenth of a gravity!—and was glad that he needed only a few lessons; doubtless his astronaut training helped. He was, the Wingmaster told him, the best pupil he had ever taught: but perhaps he said that to all of them.

After a dozen free-flights in a chamber forty meters on a side, crisscrossed with various obstacles that he easily avoided, Poole was given the all-clear for his first solo—and felt nineteen years old again, about to take off in the Flagstaff Aero Club's antique Cessna.

The unexciting name "The Aviary" had not prepared him for the venue of this maiden flight. Though it seemed even more enormous than the space holding the forests and gardens down at the lunar gee level, it was almost the same size, since it too occupied an entire floor of the gently tapering Tower. A circular void, half a kilometer high and over four kilometers wide, it appeared truly enormous, as there were no features on which the eye could rest. Because the walls were a uniform pale blue, they contributed to the impression of infinite space.

Poole had not really believed the Wingmaster's boast, "You can have any scenery you like," and intended to throw him what he was sure was an impossible challenge. But on this first flight, at the dizzy altitude of fifty meters, there were no visual distractions. Of course, a fall from the equivalent altitude of five meters in the tenfold greater Earth gravity could break one's neck; however, even minor bruises were unlikely here, as the entire floor was covered with a network of flexible cables. The whole chamber was a giant trampoline; one could, thought Poole, have a lot of fun here—even without wings.

With firm, downward strokes, Poole lifted himself into the air. In almost no time, it seemed that he was a hundred meters in the air, and still rising.

"Slow down!" said the Wingmaster. "I can't keep up with you!"

Poole straightened out, then attempted a slow roll. He felt light-headed as well as light-bodied (less than ten kilograms!) and wondered if the concentration of oxygen had been increased.

This was wonderful—quite different from zero gravity, as it posed more of a physical challenge. The nearest thing to it was scuba diving: he wished there were birds here, to emulate the equally colorful coral fish who had so often accompanied him over tropical reefs.

The Wingmaster put him through a series of maneuvers one by one—rolls, loops, upside-down flying, hovering . . . Finally he said: "Nothing more I can teach you. Now let's enjoy the view."

Just for a moment, Poole almost lost control—as he was probably expected to do. For, without the slightest warning, he was surrounded by snowcapped mountains, and was flying down a narrow pass, only meters from some unpleasantly jagged rocks.

Of course, this could not be real: those mountains were as insubstantial as clouds, and he could fly right through them if he wished. Nevertheless, he veered away from the cliff face (there was an eagle's nest on one of its ledges, holding two eggs that he felt he could touch if he came closer) and headed for more open space.

The mountains vanished; suddenly, it was night. And then the stars came out—not the miserable few thousand in the impoverished skies of Earth, but legions beyond counting. And not only stars, but the spiral whirlpools of distant galaxies, the teeming, close-packed sun-swarms of globular clusters.

There was no possible way this could be real, even if he had been magically transported to some world where such skies existed. For those galaxies were receding even as he watched; stars were fading, exploding, being born in stellar nurseries of glowing fire-mist. Every second, a million years must be passing . . .

The overwhelming spectacle disappeared as quickly as it had come:

he was back in the empty sky, alone except for his instructor, in the
featureless blue cylinder of the Aviary.

"I think that's enough for one day," said the Wingmaster, hovering
a few meters above Poole. "What scenery would you like, the next
time you come here?"

Poole did not hesitate. With a smile, he answered the question.

11. HERE BE DRAGONS

He would never have believed it possible, even with the technology of this day and age. How many terabytes—petabytes—was there a large enough word?—of information must have been accumulated over the centuries, and in what sort of storage medium? Better not think about it, and follow Indra's advice: "Forget you're an engineer—and enjoy yourself."

He was certainly enjoying himself now, though his pleasure was mixed with an almost overwhelming sense of nostalgia. For he was flying, or so it seemed, at an altitude of about two kilometers, above the spectacular and unforgotten landscape of his youth. Of course, the perspective was false, since the Aviary was only half a kilometer high, but the illusion was perfect.

He circled Meteor Crater, remembering how he had scrambled up its sides during his earlier astronaut training. How incredible that anyone could ever have doubted its origin, and the accuracy of its name! Yet well into the Twentieth Century, distinguished geologists had argued that it was volcanic: not until the coming of the space age was it—reluctantly—accepted that all planets were still under continual bombardment.

Poole was quite sure that his comfortable cruising speed was nearer twenty than two hundred kilometers an hour, yet he had been allowed to reach Flagstaff in less than fifteen minutes. And there were the whitely gleaming domes of the Lowell Observatory, which he had visited so often as a boy, and whose friendly staff had undoubtedly been responsible for his choice of career. He had sometimes wondered what his profession might have been, had he not been born in Arizona, near the very spot where the most long-enduring and influential of Martian fantasies had been created. Perhaps it was imagination, but Poole thought he could just see Lowell's unique tomb, close to the great telescope that had fueled his dreams.

From what year, and what season, had this image been captured? He guessed it had come from the spy satellites that had watched over the world of the early Twenty-first Century. It could not be much later than his own time, for the layout of the city was just as he remembered. Perhaps if he went low enough he would even see himself . . .

But he knew that was absurd; he had already discovered that this was the nearest he could get. If he flew any closer, the image would start to break up, revealing its basic pixels. It was better to keep his distance, and not destroy the beautiful illusion.

And there—it was incredible!—was the little park where he had played with his junior and high school friends. The City Fathers were always arguing about its maintenance, as the water supply became more and more critical. Well, at least it had survived to this time—whenever that might be.

And then another memory brought tears to his eyes. Along those narrow paths, whenever he could get home from Houston or the Moon, he had walked with his beloved Rhodesian Ridgeback, throwing sticks for him to retrieve, as man and dog had done from time immemorial.

Poole had hoped, with all his heart, that Rikki would still be there to greet him when he returned from Jupiter, and had left him in the care of his younger brother Martin. He almost lost control, and sank several meters before regaining stability, as he once more faced the bitter truth that both Rikki and Martin had been dust for centuries.

When he could see properly again, he noticed that the dark band of the Grand Canyon was just visible on the far horizon. He was debating whether to head for it—he was growing a little tired—when he became aware that he was not alone in the sky. Something else was approaching, and it was certainly not a human flyer. Although it was difficult to judge distances here, it seemed much too large for that.

"Well," he thought, "I'm not particularly surprised to meet a pterodactyl here—indeed, it's just the sort of thing I'd expect. I hope it's friendly—or that I can outfly it if it isn't. Oh, no!"

A pterodactyl was not a bad guess: maybe eight points out of ten. What was approaching him now, with slow flaps of its great leathery wings, was a dragon straight out of Fairyland. And, to complete the picture, there was a beautiful lady riding on its back.

At least, Poole assumed she was beautiful. The traditional image was rather spoiled by one trifling detail: much of her face was concealed by a large pair of aviator's goggles that might have come straight from the open cockpit of a World War I biplane.

Poole hovered in midair, like a swimmer treading water, until the oncoming monster came close enough for him to hear the flapping of its great wings. Even when it was less than twenty meters away, he could not decide whether it was a machine or a bio-construct: probably both.

And then he forgot about the dragon, for the rider removed her goggles.

The trouble with clichés, some philosopher remarked, probably with a yawn, is that they are so boringly true.

But "love at first sight" is never boring.

Danil could provide no information, but then Poole had not expected any from him. His ubiquitous escort—he certainly would not pass muster as a classic valet—seemed so limited in his functions that Poole sometimes wondered if he was mentally handicapped, unlikely though that seemed. He understood the functioning of all the household appliances, carried out simple orders with speed and efficiency, and knew his way about the Tower. But that was all; it was impossible to have an intelligent conversation with him, and any polite queries about his family were met with a look of blank incomprehension. Poole had even wondered if he too was a bio-robot.

Indra, however, gave him the answer he needed right away.

"Oh, you've met the Dragon Lady!"

"Is that what you call her? What's her real name—and can you get me her Ident? We were hardly in a position to touch palms."

"Of course—no problemo."

"Where did you pick up that?"

Indra looked uncharacteristically confused.

"I've no idea—some old book or movie. Is it a good figure of speech?"

"Not if you're over fifteen."

"I'll try to remember. Now tell me what happened—unless you want to make me jealous."

They were now such good friends that they could discuss any subject with perfect frankness. Indeed, they had laughingly lamented their total lack of romantic interest in each other—though Indra had once commented, "I guess that if we were both marooned on a desert asteroid, with no hope of rescue, we could come to some arrangement."

"First, you tell me who she is."

"Her name's Aurora McAuley; among many other things, she's President of the Society for Creative Anachronisms. And if you thought Draco was impressive, wait until you see some of their other—ah—creations. Like Moby Dick—and a whole zooful of dinosaurs Mother Nature never thought of."

This is too good to be true, thought Poole.

I am the biggest anachronism on Planet Earth.

12. FRUSTRATION

Until now, he had almost forgotten that conversation with the Space Agency psychologist.

"You may be gone from Earth for at least three years. If you like, I can give you a harmless anaphrodisiac implant that will last out the mission. I promise we'll more than make it up, when you get home."

"No thanks," Poole had answered, trying to keep his face straight when he continued. "I think I can handle it."

Nevertheless, he had become suspicious after the third or fourth week—and so had Dave Bowman.

"I've noticed it too," Dave said. "I bet those damn doctors put something in our diet."

Whatever that something was—if indeed it had ever existed—it was certainly long past its shelf life. Until now, Poole had been too busy to get involved in any emotional entanglements, and had politely turned down generous offers from several young (and not so young) ladies. He was not sure whether it was his physique or his fame that appealed to them: perhaps it was nothing more than simple curiosity about a man who, for all they knew, might be an ancestor from twenty or thirty generations in the past.

To Poole's delight, Mistress McAuley's Ident conveyed the information that she was currently between lovers, and he wasted no further time in contacting her. Within twenty-four hours he was pillion-riding, with his arms enjoyably around her waist. He had also learned why aviator's goggles were a good idea, for Draco was entirely robotic, and could easily cruise at a hundred klicks. Poole doubted if any real dragons had ever attained such speeds.

He was not surprised that the ever-changing landscapes below them were straight out of legend. Ali Baba had waved angrily at them, as they overtook his flying carpet, shouting, "Can't you see where you're going!" Yet he must be a long way from Baghdad, because the dreaming spires over which they now circled could only be Oxford.

Aurora confirmed his guess as she pointed down: "That's the pub— the inn—where Lewis and Tolkien used to meet their friends, the Inklings. And look at the river—that boat just coming out from the bridge—do you see the two little girls and the clergyman in it?"

"Yes," he shouted back against the gentle susurration of Draco's slipstream. "And I suppose one of them is Alice."

Aurora turned and smiled at him over her shoulder: she seemed genuinely delighted.

"Quite correct: she's an accurate replica, based on the Reverend's photos. I was afraid you wouldn't know. So many people stopped reading soon after your time."

Poole felt a glow of satisfaction.

I believe I've passed another test, he told himself smugly. Riding on Draco must have been the first. How many more, I wonder? Fighting with broadswords?

But there were no more, and the answer to the immemorial "Your place or mine?" was—Poole's.

The next morning, shaken and mortified, he contacted Professor Anderson.

"Everything was going splendidly," he lamented, "when she suddenly became hysterical and pushed me away. I was afraid I'd hurt her somehow—

"Then she called the roomlight—we'd been in darkness—and jumped out of bed. I guess I was just staring like a fool . . ." He laughed ruefully. "She was certainly worth staring at."

"I'm sure of it. Go on."

"After a few minutes she relaxed and said something I'll never be able to forget."

Anderson waited patiently for Poole to compose himself.

"She said: 'I'm really sorry, Frank. We could have had a good time. But I didn't know that you'd been—mutilated.'"

The professor looked baffled, but only for a moment.

"Oh—I understand. I'm sorry too, Frank—perhaps I should have warned you. In my thirty years of practice, I've only seen half a dozen cases—all for valid medical reasons, which certainly didn't apply to you . . .

"Circumcision made a lot of sense in primitive times—and even in your century, as a defense against some unpleasant, even fatal, diseases in backward countries with poor hygiene. But otherwise there was absolutely no excuse for it—and several arguments against, as you've just discovered!

"I checked the records after I'd examined you the first time, and found that by mid-Twenty-first Century there had been so many malpractice suits that the American Medical Association had been forced to ban it. The arguments among the contemporary doctors are very entertaining."

"I'm sure they are," said Poole morosely.

"In some countries it continued for another century: then some unknown genius coined a slogan—please excuse the vulgarity—'God designed us: circumcision is blasphemy.' That more or less ended the practice. But if you want, it would be easy to arrange a transplant— you wouldn't be making medical history, by any means."

"I don't think it would work. Afraid I'd start laughing every time."

"That's the spirit—you're already getting over it."

Somewhat to his surprise, Poole realized that Anderson's prognosis was correct. He even found himself already laughing.

"Now what, Frank?"

"Aurora's 'Society for Creative Anachronisms.' I'd hoped it would improve my chances. Just my luck to have found one anachronism she doesn't appreciate."

13. STRANGER IN A STRANGE TIME

Indra was not quite as sympathetic as he had hoped; perhaps, after all, there was some sexual jealousy in their relationship. And—much more serious—what they wryly labeled the Dragon Debacle led to their first real argument.

It began innocently enough, when Indra complained:

"People are always asking me why I've devoted my life to such a horrible period of history, and it's not much of an answer to say that there were even worse ones."

"Then why are you interested in my century?"

"Because it marks the transition between barbarism and civilization."

"Thank you. Just call me Conan."

"Conan? The only one I know is the man who created Sherlock Holmes."

"Never mind—sorry I interrupted. Of course, we in the so-called developed countries thought we were civilized. At least war wasn't respectable anymore, and the United Nations was always doing its best to stop the wars that did break out."

"Not very successfully: I'd give it about three out of ten. But what we find incredible is the way that people—right up to the early 2000s!—calmly accepted behavior we would consider atrocious. And believed in the most mind-boggled—"

"Boggling."

"—nonsense, which surely any rational person would dismiss out of hand."

"Examples, please."

"Well, your really trivial loss started me doing some research, and I was appalled by what I found. Did you know that every year in some countries thousands of little girls were hideously mutilated to preserve their virginity? Many of them died—but the authorities turned a blind eye."

"I agree that was terrible—but what could my government do about it?"

"A great deal—if it wished. But that would have offended the people who supplied it with oil—and bought its weapons, like the landmines that killed and maimed civilians by the thousands."

"You don't understand, Indra. Often we had no choice: we couldn't reform the whole world. And didn't somebody once say 'Politics is the art of the possible'?"

"Quite true—which is why only second-rate minds go into it. Genius likes to challenge the impossible."

"Well, I'm glad you have a good supply of genius, so you can put things right."

"Do I detect a hint of sarcasm? Thanks to our computers, we can run political experiments in cyberspace before trying them out in practice. Lenin was unlucky; he was born a hundred years too soon. Russian communism might have worked—at least for a while—if it had had microchips. And had managed to avoid Stalin."

Poole was constantly amazed by Indra's knowledge of his age—as well as by her ignorance of so much that he took for granted. In a way, he had the reverse problem. Even if he lived the hundred years that had been confidently promised him, he could never learn enough to feel at home. In any conversation, there would always be references he did not understand, and jokes that would go over his head. Worse still, he would always feel on the verge of some faux pas—about to create some social disaster that would embarrass even the best of his new friends . . .

. . . Such as the occasion when he was lunching, fortunately in his own quarters, with Indra and Professor Anderson. The meals that emerged from the autochef were always perfectly acceptable, having been designed to match his physiological requirements. But they were certainly nothing to get excited about, and would have been the despair of a Twenty-first-Century gourmet.

Then, one day, an unusually tasty dish appeared, which brought back vivid memories of the deer hunts and barbecues of his youth.

However, there was something unfamiliar about both flavor and texture, so Poole asked the obvious question.

Anderson merely smiled, but for a few seconds Indra looked as if she was about to be sick. Then she recovered and said: "You tell him—after we've finished eating."

Now what have I done wrong? Poole asked himself. Half an hour later, with Indra rather pointedly absorbed in a video display at the other end of the room, his knowledge of the Third Millennium made another major advance.

"Corpse-food was on the way out even in your time," Anderson explained. "Raising animals to—ugh—eat them became economically impossible. I don't know how many acres of land it took to feed one cow, but at least ten humans could survive on the plants it produced. And probably a hundred, with hydroponic techniques.

"But what finished the whole horrible business was not economics but disease. It started first with cattle, then spread to other food animals—a kind of virus, I believe, that affected the brain, and caused a particularly nasty death. Although a cure was eventually found, it was too late to turn back the clock—and anyway, synthetic foods were now far cheaper, and you could get them in any flavor you liked."

Remembering weeks of satisfying but unexciting meals, Poole had strong reservations about this. For why, he wondered, did he still have wistful dreams of spareribs and cordon bleu steaks?

Other dreams were far more disturbing, and he was afraid that before long he would have to ask Anderson for medical assistance. Despite everything that was being done to make him feel at home, the strangeness and sheer complexity of this new world was beginning to overwhelm him. During sleep, as if in an unconscious effort to escape, he often reverted to his earlier life: but when he awoke, that only made matters worse.

It had not been a good idea to travel across to America Tower and look down, in reality and not in simulation, on the landscape of his youth. With optical aid, when the atmosphere was clear, he could get so close that he could see individual human beings as they went about their affairs, sometimes along streets that he remembered . . .

And always, at the back of his mind, was the knowledge that down there had once lived everyone he had ever loved. Mother, Father (before he had gone off with that Other Woman), dear Uncle George and Aunt Lil, brother Martin—and, not least, a succession of dogs, beginning with the warm puppies of his earliest childhood and culminating in Rikki.

Above all, there was the memory—and mystery—of Helena . . .

It had begun as a casual affair, in the early days of his astrotraining, but had become more and more serious as the years went by. Just before he had left for Jupiter, they had planned to make it permanent—when he returned.

And if he did not, Helena wished to have his child. He still recalled the blend of solemnity and hilarity with which they had made the necessary arrangements . . .

Now, a thousand years later, despite all his efforts, he had been unable to find if Helena had kept her promise. Just as there were now gaps in his own memory, so there were also in the collective records of mankind. The worst was that created by the devastating electromagnetic pulse from the 2304 asteroid impact, which had wiped out several percent of the world's information banks, despite all backups and safety systems. Poole could not help wondering if the records of his own children were among all the exabytes that were irretrievably lost. Even now, his descendants of the thirtieth generation might be walking the Earth; but he would never know.

It helped a little to have discovered that—unlike Aurora—some ladies of this era did not consider him to be damaged goods. On the contrary: they often found his alteration quite exciting, but this slightly bizarre reaction made it impossible for Poole to establish any close relationship. Nor was he anxious to do so; all that he really needed was the occasional healthy, mindless exercise.

Mindless—that was the trouble. He no longer had any purpose in life. And the weight of too many memories was upon him; paraphrasing the title of a famous book he had read in his youth, he often said to himself, "I am a Stranger in a Strange Time."

There were even occasions when he looked down at the beautiful planet on which—if he obeyed doctor's orders—he could never walk again, and wondered what it would be like to make a second acquaintance with the vacuum of space. Though it was not easy to get through the airlocks without triggering some alarm, it had been done: every few years, some determined suicide made a brief meteoric display in the Earth's atmosphere.

Perhaps it was just as well that deliverance was on its way, from a completely unexpected direction.

* * *

"Nice to meet you, Commander Poole—for the second time."

"I'm sorry—don't recall—but then I see so many people."

"No need to apologize. First time was out round Neptune."

"Captain Chandler—delighted to see you! Can I get you something from the autochef?"

"Anything with over twenty percent alcohol will be fine."

"And what are you doing back on Earth? They told me you never come inside Mars orbit."

"Almost true—though I was born here, I think it's a dirty, smelly place—too many people—creeping up to a billion again!"

"More than ten billion in my time. By the way, did you get my 'Thank-you' message?"

"Yes—and I know I should have contacted you. But I waited until I headed Sunward again. So here I am. Your good health!"

As the Captain disposed of his drink with impressive speed, Poole tried to analyze his visitor. Beards—even small goatees like Chandler's—were very rare in this society, and he had never known an astronaut who wore one: they did not coexist comfortably with space helmets. Of course, a captain might go for years between EVAs, and in any case most outside jobs were done by robots; but there was always the risk of the unexpected, when one might have to get suited in a hurry. It was obvious that Chandler was something of an eccentric, and Poole's heart warmed to him.

"You've not answered my question. If you don't like Earth, what are you doing here?"

"Oh, mostly contacting old friends—it's wonderful to forget hour-long delays, and to have real-time conversations! But of course that's not the reason. My old rust bucket is having a refit, up at the Rim shipyard. And the armor has to be replaced; when it gets down to a few centimeters thick, I don't sleep too well."

"Armor?"

"Dust shield. Not such a problem in your time, was it? But it's a dirty environment out round Jupiter, and our normal cruise speed is several thousand klicks—a second! So there's a continuous gentle pattering, like raindrops on the roof."

"You're joking!"

"Course I am. If we really could hear anything, we'd be dead. Luckily, this sort of unpleasantness is very rare—last serious accident was twenty years ago. We know all the main comet streams, where most of the junk is, and are careful to avoid them—except when we're match-ing velocity to round up ice.

"But why don't you come aboard and have a look around, before we take off for Jupiter?"

"I'd be delighted . . . did you say Jupiter?"

"Well, Ganymede, of course—Anubis City. We've a lot of business there, and several of us have families they haven't seen for months."

Poole scarcely heard him.

Suddenly—unexpectedly—and perhaps none too soon, he had found a reason for living.

Commander Frank Poole was the sort of man who hated to leave a job undone—and a few specks of cosmic dust, even moving at a thou-sand kilometers a second, were not likely to discourage him.

He had unfinished business at the world once known as Jupiter.

II. GOLIATH

14. A FAREWELL TO EARTH

"Anything you want—within reason" he had been told. Frank Poole was not sure if his hosts would consider that returning to Jupiter was a reasonable request; indeed, he was not quite sure himself, and was beginning to have second thoughts.

He had already committed himself to scores of engagements, weeks in advance. Most of them he would be happy to miss, but there were some he would be sorry to forgo. In particular, he hated to disappoint the senior class from his old high school—how astonishing that it still existed!—when they planned to visit him next month.

However, he was relieved—and a little surprised—when both Indra and Professor Anderson agreed that it was an excellent idea. For the first time, he realized that they had been concerned with his mental health; perhaps a holiday from Earth would be the best possible cure.

And, most important of all, Captain Chandler was delighted. "You can have my cabin," he promised. "I'll kick the First Mate out of hers." There were times when Poole wondered if Chandler, with his beard and swagger, was not another anachronism. He could easily picture him on the bridge of a battered three-master, with skull and crossbones flying overhead.

Once his decision had been made, events moved with surprising speed. He had accumulated very few possessions, and fewer still that he needed to take with him. The most important was Miss Pringle, his electronic alter ego and secretary, now the storehouse of both his lives, and the small stack of terabyte memories that went with her.

Miss Pringle was not much larger than the handheld personal assistants of his own age, and usually lived, like the Old West's Colt 45, in a quick-draw holster at his waist. She could communicate with him by audio or Braincap, and her prime duty was to act as an information filter and a buffer to the outside world. Like any good secretary, she knew when to reply, in the appropriate format: "I'll put you through now" or, much more frequently: "I'm sorry—Mr. Poole is engaged. Please record your message and he will get back to you as soon as possible." Usually, this was never.

There were very few farewells to be made: though real-time conversations would be impossible owing to the sluggish velocity of radio waves, he would be in constant touch with Indra and Joe—the only genuine friends he had made.

Somewhat to his surprise, Poole realized that he would miss his enigmatic but useful "valet," because he would now have to handle all the small chores of everyday life by himself. Danil bowed slightly when they parted, but otherwise showed no sign of emotion, as they took the long ride up to the outer curve of the world-circling wheel, thirty-six thousand kilometers above central Africa.

"I'm not sure, Dim, that you'll appreciate the comparison. But do you know what *Goliath* reminds me of?"

They were now such good friends that Poole could use the Captain's nickname—but only when no one else was around.

"Something unflattering, I assume."

"Not really. But when I was a boy, I came across a whole pile of old science-fiction magazines that my uncle George had abandoned— 'pulps,' they were called, after the cheap paper they were printed on . . . most of them were already falling to bits. They had wonderful garish covers, showing strange planets and monsters—and, of course, spaceships!

"As I grew older, I realized how ridiculous those spaceships were. They were usually rocket-driven—but there was never any sign of propellant tanks! Some of them had rows of windows from stem to stern, just like ocean liners. There was one favorite of mine with a huge glass dome—a space-going conservatory . . .

"Well, those old artists had the last laugh; too bad they could never know. *Goliath* looks more like their dreams than the flying fuel-tanks we used to launch from the Cape. Your inertial drive still seems too good to be true—no visible means of support, unlimited range and speed . . . sometimes I think I'm the one who's dreaming!"

Chandler laughed and pointed to the view outside.

"Does that look like a dream?"

It was the first time that Poole had seen a genuine horizon since he had come to Star City, and it was not quite as far away as he had expected. After all, he was on the outer rim of a wheel seven times the diameter of Earth, so surely the view across the roof of this artificial world should extend for several hundred kilometers . . .

He used to be good at mental arithmetic—a rare achievement even in his time, and probably much rarer now. The formula to give the horizon distance was a simple one: the square root of twice your height times the radius—the sort of thing you never forgot, even if you wanted to . . .

Let's see—we're about eight meters up—so root sixteen—this is easy!—say big R is forty thousand—knock off those three zeros to make it all klicks—four times root forty—hmm—just over twenty-five . . .

Well, twenty-five kilometers was a fair distance, and certainly no spaceport on Earth had ever seemed this huge. Even knowing perfectly well what to expect, it was uncanny to watch vessels many times the size of his long-lost *Discovery* lifting off, not only with no sound, but with no apparent means of propulsion. Though Poole missed the flame and fury of the old-time countdowns, he had to admit that this was cleaner, more efficient—and far safer.

Strangest of all, though, was to sit up here on the Rim, in the Geostationary Orbit itself—and to feel weight! Just meters away, outside the window of the tiny observation lounge, servicing robots and a few space-suited humans were gliding gently about their business; yet here inside *Goliath* the inertial field was maintaining standard Mars gee.

"Sure you don't want to change your mind, Frank?" Captain Chandler had asked jokingly, as he left for the bridge. "Still ten minutes before liftoff."

"Wouldn't be very popular if I did, would I? No—as they used to say back in the old days—we have commit. Ready or not, here I come."

Poole felt the need to be alone when the drive went on, and the tiny crew—only four men and three women—respected his wish. Perhaps they guessed how he must be feeling, to leave Earth for the second time in a thousand years—and, once again, to face an unknown destiny.

Jupiter–Lucifer was on the other side of the Sun, and the almost straight-line of *Goliath*'s orbit would take them close to Venus. Poole looked forward to seeing, with his own unaided eyes, if Earth's sister planet was now beginning to live up to that description, after centuries of terraforming.

From a thousand kilometers up, Star City looked like a gigantic metal band around Earth's equator, dotted with gantries, pressure domes, scaffolding holding half-completed ships, antennas, and other more enigmatic structures. It was diminishing swiftly as *Goliath* headed Sunward, and presently Poole could see how incomplete it was: there were huge gaps spanned only by a spider's web of scaffolding, which would probably never be completely enclosed.

And now they were falling below the plane of the ring; it was midwinter in the Northern Hemisphere, so the slim halo of Star City was inclined at over twenty degrees to the Sun. Already Poole could see the American and Asian Towers, as shining threads stretching outward and away, beyond the blue haze of the atmosphere.

He was barely conscious of time as *Goliath* gained speed, moving more swiftly than any comet that had ever fallen Sunward from interstellar space. The Earth, almost full, still spanned his field of view, and he could now see the full length of the Africa Tower that had been his home in the life he was now leaving—perhaps, he could not help thinking, forever.

When they were fifty thousand kilometers out, he was about to view the whole of Star City, as a narrow ellipse enclosing the Earth. Though the far side was barely visible, as a hairline of light against the stars, it was awe-inspiring to think that the human race had now set this sign upon the heavens.

Then Poole remembered the rings of Saturn, infinitely more glorious. The astronautical engineers still had a long, long way to go, before they could match the achievements of Nature.

Or, if that was the right word, Deus.

15. TRANSIT OF VENUS

When he woke the next morning, they were already at Venus. But the huge, dazzling crescent of the still cloud-wrapped planet was not the most striking object in the sky: *Goliath* was floating above an endless expanse of crinkled silver foil, flashing in the sunlight with ever-changing patterns as the ship drifted across it.

Poole remembered that in his own age there had been an artist who had wrapped whole buildings in plastic sheets: how he would have loved this opportunity to package billions of tons of ice in a glittering envelope! Only in this way could the core of a comet be protected from evaporation on its decades-long journey Sunward.

"You're in luck, Frank," Chandler had told him. "This is something I've never seen myself. It should be spectacular. Impact due in just over an hour. We've given it a little nudge, to make sure it comes down in the right place. Don't want anyone to get hurt."

Poole looked at him in astonishment.

"You mean—there are already people on Venus?"

"About fifty mad scientists, near the South Pole. Of course, they're well dug in, but we should shake them up a bit—even though Ground Zero is on the other side of the planet. Or I should say 'Atmosphere Zero'—it will be days before anything except the shock wave gets down to the surface."

As the cosmic iceberg, sparkling and flashing in its protective envelope, dwindled away toward Venus, Poole was struck with a sudden, poignant memory. The Christmas trees of his childhood had been adorned with just such ornaments, delicate bubbles of colored glass.

And the comparison was not completely ludicrous: for many families on Earth, this was still the right season for gifts, and *Goliath* was bringing a present beyond price to another world.

The radar image of the tortured Venusian landscape—its weird volcanoes, pancake domes, and narrow, sinuous canyons—dominated the main screen of *Goliath*'s control center, but Poole preferred the evidence of his own eyes. Although the unbroken sea of clouds that covered the planet revealed nothing of the inferno beneath, he wanted to see what would happen when the stolen comet struck. In a matter of seconds, the myriads of tons of frozen hydrates that had been gathering speed for decades on the downhill run from Neptune would deliver all their energy . . .

The initial flash was even brighter than he had expected. How strange that a missile made of ice could generate temperatures that must be in the tens of thousands of degrees! Though the filters of the viewport would have absorbed all the dangerous shorter wavelengths, the fierce blue of the fireball proclaimed that it was hotter than the sun.

It was cooling rapidly as it expanded—through yellow, orange, red . . . The shock wave would now be spreading outward at the velocity of sound—and what a sound that must be!—so in a few minutes there should be some visible indication of its passage across the face of Venus.

And there it was! Only a tiny black ring—like an insignificant puff of smoke, giving no hint of the cyclonic fury that must be blasting its way outward from the point of impact. As Poole watched, it slowly expanded, though owing to its scale there was no sense of visible movement: he had to wait for a full minute before he could be quite sure that it had grown larger.

After a quarter of an hour, however, it was the most prominent marking on the planet. Though much fainter—a dirty gray, rather than black—the shock wave was now a ragged circle more than a thousand kilometers across. Poole guessed that it had lost its original symmetry while sweeping over the great mountain ranges that lay beneath it.

Captain Chandler's voice sounded briskly over the ship's address system.

"Putting you through to Aphrodite Base. Glad to say they're not shouting for help—"

"—shook us up a bit, but just what we expected. Monitors indicate some rain already over the Nokomis Mountains—it will soon evaporate, but that's a beginning. And there seems to have been a flash flood in Hecate Chasm—too good to be true, but we're checking. There was a temporary lake of boiling water there after the last delivery—"

I don't envy them, Poole told himself, but I certainly admire them. They prove that the spirit of adventure still exists in this perhaps-too-comfortable and well-adjusted society.

"—and thanks again for bringing this little load down in the right place. With any luck—and if we can get that sunscreen up into sync orbit—we'll have some permanent seas before long. And then we can plant coral reefs, to make lime and pull the excess CO_2 out of the atmosphere . . . hope I live to see it!"

I hope you do, thought Poole in silent admiration. He had often dived in the tropical seas of Earth, admiring weird and colorful creatures often so bizarre that it was hard to believe anything stranger would be found, even on the planets of other suns.

"Package delivered on time, and receipt acknowledged," said Captain Chandler with obvious satisfaction. "Goodbye Venus—Ganymede, here we come."

MISS PRINGLE

FILE—WALLACE

Hello, Indra. Yes, you were quite right. I do miss our little arguments. Chandler and I get along fine, and at first the crew treated me—this will amuse you—rather like a holy relic. But they're beginning to accept me, and have even started to pull my leg (do you know that idiom?).

It's annoying not to be able to have a real conversation—we've crossed the orbit of Mars, so radio round-trip is already over an hour. But there's one advantage—you won't be able to interrupt me . . .

Even though it will take us only a week to reach Jupiter, I thought I'd have time to relax. Not a bit of it: my fingers started to itch, and I couldn't resist going back to school. So I've begun basic training, all over again, in one of *Goliath*'s minishuttles. Maybe Dim will actually let me solo . . .

It's not much bigger than *Discovery*'s pods—but what a difference! First of all, of course, it doesn't use rockets: I can't get used to the luxury of the inertial drive, and unlimited range. Could fly back to Earth if I had to—though I'd probably get—remember the phrase I used once, and you guessed its meaning?—"stir crazy."

The biggest difference, though, is the control system. It's been a big challenge for me to get used to hands-off operation—and the computer has had to learn to recognize my voice commands. At first it was asking every five minutes, "Do you really mean that?" I know it would be better to use the Braincap—but I'm still not completely confident with that gadget. Not sure if I'll ever get used to something reading my mind . . .

By the way, the shuttle's called *Falcon*. It's a nice name—and I was disappointed to find that no one aboard knew that it goes all the way back to the Apollo missions, when we first landed on the Moon . . .

Uh huh—there was a lot more I wanted to say, but the skipper is calling. Back to the classroom—love and out.

STORE

TRANSMIT

Hello Frank—Indra calling—if that's right word!—on my new Thoughtwriter—old one had nervous breakdown ha ha—so be lots of mistakes—no time to edit before I send. Hope you can make sense.

COMSET! Channel one oh three—record from twelve thirty—correction—thirteen thirty. Sorry . . .

Hope I can get old unit fixed—knew all my shortcuts and abbreves—maybe should get psychoanalyzed like in your time—never understood how that Fraudian—mean Freudian ha ha—nonsense lasted as long as it did—

Reminds me—came across late 20th defin other day—may amuse you—something like this—quote—Psychoanalysis—contagious disease originating Vienna circa 1900—now extinct in Europe but occasional outbreaks among rich Americans. Unquote. Funny?

Sorry again—trouble with Thoughtwriters—hard to stick to point—
xz 12L w888 8***** js9812yebdc DAMN . . . STOP . . .
BACKUP

Did I do something wrong then? Will try again.

You mentioned Danil . . . sorry we always evaded your questions about him—knew you were curious, but we had very good reason—remember you once called him a nonperson? . . . not bad guess . . . !

Once you asked me about crime nowadays—I said any such interest pathological—maybe prompted by the endless sickening television programs of your time—never able to watch more than few minutes myself . . . disgusting!

DOOR—ACKNOWLEDGE!—OH, HELLO MELINDA—EXCUSE—SIT DOWN—NEARLY FINISHED . . .

Yes—crime. Always some . . . Society's irreducible noise level. What to do?

Your solution—prisons. State-sponsored perversion factories—costing ten times average family income to hold one inmate! Utterly crazy . . . Obviously something very wrong with people who shouted loudest for more prisons—they should be psychoanalyzed! But let's be fair—really no alternative before electronic monitoring and control perfected—you should see the joyful crowds smashing the prison walls then—nothing like it since Berlin fifty years earlier!

Yes—Danil. I don't know what his crime was—wouldn't tell you if I did—but presume his psych profile suggested he'd make a good— what was the word?—ballet—no, valet. Very hard to get people for some jobs—don't know how we'd manage if crime level zero! Anyway hope he's soon decontrolled and back in normal society.

SORRY MELINDA—NEARLY FINISHED.

That's it, Frank—regards to Dimitri—you must be halfway to Ganymede now—wonder if they'll ever repeal Einstein so we can talk across space in real time!

Hope this machine soon gets used to me. Otherwise be looking round for genuine antique 20th-Century word processor . . . Would you believe—once even mastered that QWERTYUIOP nonsense, which you took a couple of hundred years to get rid of?

Love and goodbye.

Hello Frank—here I am again. Still waiting acknowledgment of my last . . .

Strange you should be heading toward Ganymede, and my old friend Ted Khan. But perhaps it's not such a coincidence: he was drawn by the same enigma that you were . . .

First I must tell you something about him. His parents played a dirty trick, giving him the name Theodore. That shortens—don't ever call him that!—to Theo. See what I mean?

Can't help wondering if that's what drives him. Don't know anyone else who's developed such an interest in religion—no, obsession. Better warn you; he can be quite a bore.

By the way, how am I doing? I miss my old Thoughtwriter, but seem to be getting this machine under control. Haven't made any bad—what did you call them?—bloopers—glitches—fluffs—so far at least—

Not sure I should tell you this, in case you accidentally blurt it out, but my private nickname for Ted is "The Last Jesuit." You must know something about them—the Order was still very active in your time.

Amazing people—often great scientists—superb scholars—did a tremendous amount of good as well as much harm. One of history's supreme ironies—sincere and brilliant seekers of knowledge and truth, yet their whole philosophy hopelessly distorted by superstition . . .

Xuedn2k3jn deer 21 eidj dwpp

Damn. Got emotional and lost control. One, two, three, four . . . now is the time for all good men to come to the aid of the party . . . that's better.

Anyway, Ted has that same brand of high-minded determination; don't get into any arguments with him—he'll go over you like a steamroller.

By the way what were steamrollers? Used for pressing clothes? Can see how that could be very uncomfortable . . .

Trouble with Thoughtwriters . . . too easy to go off in all directions, no matter how hard you try to discipline yourself . . . something to be said for keyboards after all . . . sure I've said that before . . .

Ted Khan . . . Ted Khan . . . Ted Khan

He's still famous back on Earth for at least two of his sayings: "Civilization and Religion are incompatible" and "Faith is believing what you know isn't true." Actually, I don't think the last one is original; if it is, that's the nearest he ever got to a joke. He never cracked a smile when I tried one of my favorites on him—hope you haven't heard it before . . . it obviously dates from your time . . .

The Dean's complaining to his Faculty. "Why do you scientists need such expensive equipment? Why can't you be like the Math Department, which only needs a blackboard and a wastepaper basket? Better still, like the Department of Philosophy. That doesn't even need a wastepaper basket . . ." Well, perhaps Ted had heard it before . . . I expect most philosophers have . . .

Anyway, give him my regards—and don't, repeat don't, get into any arguments with him!

Love and best wishes from Africa Tower.

TRANSCRIBE. STORE.

TRANSMIT—POOLE

16. THE CAPTAIN'S TABLE

The arrival of such a distinguished passenger had caused a certain disruption in the tight little world of *Goliath*, but the crew had adapted to it with good humor. Every day, at 18.00 hours, all personnel gathered for dinner in the wardroom, which under zero-gee could hold at least thirty people in comfort, if spread uniformly around the walls. However, most of the time the ship's working areas were held at lunar gravity, so there was an undeniable floor—and more than eight bodies made a crowd.

The semi-circular table that unfolded around the autochef at mealtimes could just seat the entire seven-person crew, with the Captain at the place of honor. One extra created such insuperable problems that somebody now had to eat alone for every meal. After much good-natured debate, it was decided to make the choice in alphabetical order—not of proper names, which were hardly ever used, but of nicknames. It had taken Poole some time to get used to them: "Bolts" (structural engineering); "Chips" (computers and communications); "First" (First Mate); "Life" (medical and life-support systems); "Props" (propulsion and power); and "Stars" (orbits and navigation).

During the ten-day voyage, as he listened to the stories, jokes, and complaints of his temporary shipmates, Poole learned more about the Solar System than during his months on Earth. All aboard were obviously delighted to have a new and perhaps naive listener as an attentive one-man audience, but Poole was seldom taken in by their more imaginative stories.

Yet sometimes it was hard to know where to draw the line. No one really believed in the Golden Asteroid, which was usually regarded as a Twenty-fourth-Century hoax. But what about the Mercurian plasmoids, which had been reported by at least a dozen reliable witnesses during the last five hundred years?

The simplest explanation was that they were related to ball lightning, responsible for so many "Unidentified Flying Object" reports on Earth and Mars. But some observers swore that they had shown purposefulness—even inquisitiveness—when they were encountered at close quarters. Nonsense, answered the skeptics—merely electrostatic attraction!

Inevitably, this led to discussions about life in the Universe, and Poole found himself—not for the first time—defending his own era against its extremes of credulity and skepticism. Although the "Aliens are among us" mania had already subsided when he was a boy, even as late as the 2020s the Space Agency was still plagued by lunatics who claimed to have been contacted—or abducted—by visitors from other worlds. Their delusions had been reinforced by sensational media exploitation, and the whole syndrome was later enshrined in the medical literature as "Adamski's Disease."

The discovery of TMA-1 had, paradoxically, put an end to this sorry nonsense, by demonstrating that though there was indeed intelligence elsewhere, it had apparently not concerned itself with mankind for several million years. TMA-1 had also convincingly refuted the handful of scientists who argued that life above the bacterial level was such an improbable phenomenon that the human race was alone in this Galaxy—if not the Cosmos.

Goliath's crew was more interested in the technology than the politics and economics of Poole's era, and was particularly fascinated by the revolution that had taken place in his own lifetime: the end of the fossil fuel age, triggered by the harnessing of vacuum energy. They found it hard to imagine the smog-choked cities of the Twentieth Century, and the waste, greed, and appalling environmental disasters of the Oil Age.

"Don't blame me," said Poole, fighting back gamely after one round of criticism. "Anyway, see what a mess the Twenty-first Century made."

There was a chorus of "What do you mean?"'s around the table.

"Well, as soon as the so-called Age of Infinite Power got under way, and everyone had thousands of kilowatts of cheap, clean energy to play with—you know what happened!"

"Oh, you mean the Thermal Crisis. But that was fixed."

"Eventually—after you'd covered half the Earth with reflectors to bounce the sun's heat back into space. Otherwise it would have been as parboiled as Venus by now."

The crew's knowledge of Third Millennium history was so surprisingly limited that Poole—thanks to the intensive education he had received in Star City—could often amaze them with details of events centuries after his own time. However, he was flattered to discover how well acquainted they were with *Discovery*'s log; it had become one of the classic records of the Space Age. They looked on it as he might have regarded a Viking saga; often he had to remind himself that he was midway in time between *Goliath* and the first ships to cross the western ocean.

"On your Day 86," Stars reminded him, at dinner on the fifth evening, "you passed within two thousand kay of asteroid 7794—and shot a probe into it. Do you remember?"

"Of course I do," Poole answered rather brusquely. "To me, it happened less than a year ago."

"Um: sorry. Well, tomorrow we'll be even closer to 13, 445. Like to have a look? With autoguidance and freeze-frame, we should have a window all of ten milliseconds wide."

A hundredth of a second! That few minutes in *Discovery* had seemed hectic enough, but now everything would happen fifty times faster . . .

"How large is it?" Poole asked.

"Thirty by twenty by fifteen meters," Stars replied. "Looks like a battered brick."

"Sorry we don't have a slug to fire at it," said Props. "Did you ever wonder if 7794 would hit back?"

"Never occurred to us. But it did give the astronomers a lot of useful information, so it was worth the risk . . . Anyway, a hundredth of a second hardly seems worth the bother. Thanks all the same."

"I understand. When you've seen one asteroid, you've seen them—"

"Not true, Chips. When I was on Eros—"

"As you've told us at least a dozen times—"

Poole's mind tuned out the discussion, so that it was a background of meaningless noise. He was a thousand years in the past, recalling the only excitement of *Discovery*'s mission before the final disaster. Though he and Bowman were perfectly aware that 7794 was merely a lifeless, airless chunk of rock, that knowledge scarcely affected their feelings. It was the only solid matter they would meet this side of Jupiter, and they had stared at it with the emotions of sailors on a long sea voyage, skirting a coast on which they could not land.

It was turning slowly end over end, and there were mottled patches of light and shade distributed at random over its surface. Sometimes it sparkled like a distant window, as planes or outcroppings of crystalline material flashed in the sun . . .

He remembered, also, the mounting tension as they waited to see if their aim had been accurate. It was not easy to hit such a small target, two thousand kilometers away, moving at a relative velocity of twenty kilometers a second.

Then, against the darkened portion of the asteroid, there had been a sudden, dazzling explosion of light. The tiny slug—pure Uranium 238—had impacted at meteoric speed: in a fraction of a second, all its kinetic energy had been transformed into heat. A puff of incandescent gas had erupted briefly into space, and *Discovery*'s cameras were recording the rapidly fading spectral lines, looking for the telltale signatures of glowing atoms. A few hours later, back on Earth, the astronomers learned for the first time the composition of an asteroid's crust. There were no major surprises, but several bottles of champagne changed hands.

Captain Chandler himself took little part in the very democratic discussions around his semi-circular table: he seemed content to let his crew relax and express their feelings in this informal atmosphere. There was only one unspoken rule: no serious business at mealtimes. If there were any technical or operational problems, they had to be dealt with elsewhere.

Poole had been surprised—and a little shocked—to discover that the crew's knowledge of *Goliath*'s systems was very superficial. Often he had asked questions that should have been easily answered, only to be referred to the ship's own memory banks. After a while, however, he realized that the sort of in-depth training he had received in his day was no longer possible: far too many complex systems were involved for any one man or woman to master. The various specialists merely had to know what their equipment did, not how. Reliability depended on redundancy and automatic checking, and human intervention was much more likely to do harm than good.

Fortunately, none was required on this voyage: it had been as uneventful as any skipper could have hoped, when the new sun of Lucifer dominated the sky ahead.

III. THE WORLDS OF GALILEO

(Extract, text only, *Tourist's Guide to Outer Solar System*, v. 219.3)

Even today, the giant satellites of what was once Jupiter present us with major mysteries. Why are four worlds, orbiting the same primary and very similar in size, so different in most other respects?

Only in the case of Io, the innermost satellite, is there a convincing explanation. It is so close to Jupiter that the gravitational tides constantly kneading its interior generate colossal quantities of heat—so much, indeed, that Io's surface is semi-molten. It is the most volcanically active world in the Solar System; maps of Io have a half-life of only a few decades.

Though no permanent human bases have ever been established in such an unstable environment, there have been numerous landings and there is continuous robot monitoring. (For the tragic fate of the 2571 Expedition, see *Beagle 5*.)

Europa, second in distance from Jupiter, was originally entirely covered in ice, and showed few surface features except a complicated network of cracks. The tidal forces that dominate Io were much less powerful here, but produced enough heat to give Europa a global ocean of liquid water, in which many strange life-forms have evolved. (See Spacecraft *Tsien, Galaxy, Universe*.) Since the conversion of

Jupiter into the mini-sun Lucifer, virtually all of Europa's ice cover has melted, and extensive volcanism has created several small islands.

As is well known, there have been no landings on Europa for almost a thousand years, but the satellite is under continuous surveillance.

Ganymede, largest moon in the Solar System (diameter 5260 kilometers), has also been affected by the creation of a new sun, and its equatorial regions are warm enough to sustain terrestrial life-forms, though it does not yet have a breathable atmosphere. Most of its population is actively engaged in terraforming and scientific research; the main settlement is Anubis City (pop. 41,000), near the South Pole.

Callisto is again wholly different. Its entire surface is covered by impact craters of all sizes, so numerous that they overlap. The bombardment must have continued for millions of years, for the newer craters have completely obliterated the earlier ones. There is no permanent base on Callisto, but several automatic stations have been established there.

17. GANYMEDE

It was unusual for Frank Poole to oversleep, but he had been kept awake by strange dreams. Past and present were inextricably mixed; sometimes he was on *Discovery*, sometimes in the Africa Tower—and sometimes he was a boy again, amongst friends he had thought long forgotten.

Where am I? he asked himself as he struggled up to consciousness, like a swimmer trying to get back to the surface. There was a small window just above his bed, covered by a curtain not thick enough to completely block the light from outside. There had been a time, around the mid-Twentieth Century, when aircraft had been slow enough to feature First-Class sleeping accommodations: Poole had never sampled this nostalgic luxury, which some tourist organizations had still advertised in his own day, but he could easily imagine that he was doing so now.

He drew the curtain and looked out. No, he had not awakened in the skies of Earth, though the landscape unrolling below was not unlike the Antarctic. But the South Pole had never boasted two suns, both rising at once as *Goliath* swept toward them.

The ship was orbiting less than a hundred kilometers above what appeared to be an immense plowed field, lightly dusted with snow. But the plowman must have been drunk—or the guidance system must have gone crazy—for the furrows meandered in every direction, sometimes cutting across each other or turning back on themselves. Here and there the terrain was dotted with faint circles—ghost craters from meteor impacts aeons ago.

So this is Ganymede, Poole wondered drowsily. Mankind's farthest outpost from home! Why should any sensible person want to live here? Well, I've often thought that when I've flown over Greenland or Iceland in wintertime . . .

There was a knock on the door, a "Mind if I come in?," and Captain Chandler did so without waiting for a reply.

"Thought we'd let you sleep until we landed—that end-of-trip party did last longer than I'd intended, but I couldn't risk a mutiny by cutting it short."

Poole laughed.

"Has there ever been a mutiny in space?"

"Oh, quite a few—but not in my time. Now we've mentioned the subject, you might say that Hal started the tradition . . . sorry—perhaps I shouldn't—look—there's Ganymede City!"

Coming up over the horizon was what appeared to be a crisscross pattern of streets and avenues intersecting almost at right angles but with the slight irregularity typical of any settlement that had grown by accretion, without central planning. It was bisected by a broad river— Poole recalled that the equatorial regions of Ganymede were now warm enough for liquid water to exist—and it reminded him of an old woodcut he had seen of medieval London.

Then he noticed that Chandler was looking at him with an expression of amusement . . . and the illusion vanished as he realized the scale of the "city."

"The Ganymedeans," he said dryly, "must have been rather large, to have made roads five or ten kilometers wide."

"Twenty in some places. Impressive, isn't it? And all the result of ice stretching and contracting. Mother Nature is ingenious . . . I could show you some patterns that look even more artificial, though they're not as large as this one."

"When I was a boy, there was a big fuss about a face on Mars. Of course, it turned out to be a hill that had been carved by sandstorms . . . lots of similar ones in Earth's deserts."

"Didn't someone say that history always repeats itself? Same sort of nonsense happened with Ganymede City—some nuts claimed it had been built by aliens. But I'm afraid it won't be around much longer."

"Why?" asked Poole in surprise.

"It's already started to collapse, as Lucifer melts the permafrost. You won't recognize Ganymede in another hundred years . . .

there's the edge of Lake Gilgamesh—if you look carefully—over on the right—"

"I see what you mean. What's happening—surely the water's not boiling, even at this low pressure?"

"Electrolysis plant. Don't know how many skillions of kilograms of oxygen a day. Of course, the hydrogen goes up and gets lost—we hope."

Chandler's voice trailed off into silence. Then he resumed, in an unusually diffident tone: "All that beautiful water down there—Ganymede doesn't need half of it! Don't tell anyone, but I've been working out ways of getting some to Venus."

"Easier than nudging comets?"

"As far as energy is concerned, yes—Ganymede's escape velocity is only three klicks per second. And much, much quicker—years instead of decades. But there are a few practical difficulties . . ."

"I can appreciate that. Would you shoot it off by a mass-launcher?"

"Oh no—I'd use towers reaching up through the atmosphere, like the ones on Earth, but much smaller. We'd pump the water up to the top, freeze it down to near absolute zero, and let Ganymede sling it off in the right direction as it rotated. There would be some evaporation loss in transit, but most of it would arrive—what's so funny?"

"Sorry—I'm not laughing at the idea—it makes good sense. But you've brought back such a vivid memory. We used to have a garden sprinkler driven round and round by its water jets. What you're planning is the same thing—on a slightly bigger scale . . . using a whole world . . ."

Suddenly, another image from his past obliterated all else. Poole remembered how, in those hot Arizona days, he and Rikki had loved to chase each other through the clouds of moving mist, from the slowly revolving spray of the garden sprinkler.

Captain Chandler was a much more sensitive man than he pretended to be: he knew when it was time to leave.

"Gotta get back to the bridge," he said gruffly. "See you when we land at Anubis."

18. GRAND HOTEL

The Grand Ganymede Hotel—inevitably known throughout the Solar System as "Hotel Grannymede"—was certainly not grand, and would be lucky to get a rating of one and a half stars on Earth. As the nearest competition was several hundred million kilometers away, the management felt little need to exert itself unduly.

Yet Poole had no complaints, though he often wished that Danil was still around, to help him with the mechanics of life and to communicate more efficiently with the semi-intelligent devices with which he was surrounded. He had known a brief moment of panic when the door had closed behind the (human) bellboy, who had apparently been too awed by his famous guest to explain how any of the room's services functioned. After five minutes of fruitless talking to the unresponsive walls, Poole had finally made contact with a system that understood his accent and his commands. What an "All Worlds" news item it would have made: HISTORIC ASTRONAUT STARVES TO DEATH, TRAPPED IN GANYMEDE HOTEL ROOM!

And there would have been a double irony. Perhaps the naming of the Grannymede's only luxury suite was inevitable, but it had been a real shock to meet an ancient life-size holo of his old shipmate, in full dress uniform, as he was led into—the Bowman Suite. Poole even recognized the image: his own official portrait had been made at the same time, a few days before the mission began.

He soon discovered that most of his *Goliath* crewmates had domestic arrangements in Anubis, and were anxious for him to meet their Significant Others during the ship's planned twenty-day stop. Almost immediately he was caught up in the social and professional life of this frontier settlement, and it was Africa Tower that now seemed a distant dream.

Like many Americans, in their secret hearts, Poole had a nostalgic affection for small communities where everyone knew everyone else—in the real world, and not the virtual one of cyberspace. Anubis, with a resident population less than that of his remembered Flagstaff, was not a bad approximation of this ideal.

The three main pressure domes, each two kilometers in diameter, stood on a plateau overlooking an ice field that stretched unbroken to the horizon. Ganymede's second sun—once known as Jupiter—would never give sufficient heat to melt the polar caps. This was the principal reason for establishing Anubis in such an inhospitable spot: the city's foundations were not likely to collapse for at least several centuries.

And inside the domes, it was easy to be completely indifferent to the outside world. Poole, when he had mastered the mechanisms of the Bowman Suite, discovered that he had a limited but impressive choice of environments. He could sit beneath the palm trees on a Pacific beach, listening to the gentle murmur of the waves or, if he preferred, the roar of a tropical hurricane. He could fly slowly along the peaks of the Himalayas or down the immense canyons of Mariner Valley. He could walk through the gardens of Versailles or down the streets of half a dozen great cities, at several widely spaced times in their history. Even if the Hotel Grannymede was not one of the Solar System's most highly acclaimed resorts, it boasted facilities that would have astounded all its more famous predecessors on Earth.

But it was ridiculous to indulge in terrestrial nostalgia, when he had come halfway across the Solar System to visit a strange new world. After some experimenting, Poole arranged a compromise, for enjoyment—and inspiration—during his steadily fewer moments of leisure.

To his great regret, he had never been to Egypt, so it was delightful to relax beneath the gaze of the Sphinx—as it was before its controversial "restoration"—and to watch tourists scrambling up the massive blocks of the Great Pyramid. The illusion was perfect, apart from the no-man's-land where the desert clashed with the (slightly worn) carpet of the Bowman Suite.

The sky, however, was one that no human eyes had seen until five thousand years after the last stone was laid at Giza. But it was not an illusion; it was the complex and ever-changing reality of Ganymede.

Because this world—like its companions—had been robbed of its spin aeons ago by the tidal drag of Jupiter, the new sun born from the giant planet hung motionless in its sky. One side of Ganymede was in perpetual Lucifer-light, and although the other hemisphere was often referred to as the "Night Land," that designation was as misleading as the much earlier phrase "the dark side of the Moon." Like the lunar Farside, Ganymede's "Night Land" had the brilliant light of old Sol for half of its long day.

By a coincidence more confusing than useful, Ganymede took almost exactly one week—seven days, three hours—to orbit its primary. Attempts to create a "One Mede day = one Earth week" calendar had generated so much chaos that they had been abandoned centuries ago. Like all the other residents of the Solar System, the locals employed Universal Time, identifying their twenty-four-hour standard days by numbers rather than names.

Since Ganymede's newborn atmosphere was still extremely thin and almost cloudless, the parade of heavenly bodies provided a never-ending spectacle. At their closest, Io and Callisto each appeared about half the size of the Moon as seen from Earth—but that was the only thing they had in common. Io was so close to Lucifer that it took less than two days to race around its orbit, and showed visible movement even in a matter of minutes. Callisto, at over four times Io's distance, required two Mede days—or sixteen Earth ones—to complete its leisurely circuit.

The physical contrast between the two worlds was even more remarkable. Deep-frozen Callisto had been almost unchanged by Jupiter's conversion into a mini-sun: it was still a wasteland of shallow ice craters, so closely packed that there was not a single spot on the entire satellite that had escaped from multiple impacts, in the days when Jupiter's enormous gravity field was competing with Saturn's to gather up the debris of the outer Solar System. Since then, apart from a few stray shots, nothing had happened for several billion years.

On Io, something was happening every week. As a local wit had remarked, before the creation of Lucifer it had been Hell—now it was Hell warmed up.

Often, Poole would zoom into that burning landscape and look into the sulfurous throats of volcanoes that were continually reshaping an area larger than Africa. Sometimes incandescent fountains would soar briefly hundreds of kilometers into space, like gigantic trees of fire growing on a lifeless world.

As the floods of molten sulfur spread out from volcanoes and vents, the versatile element changed through a narrow spectrum of reds and oranges and yellows when, chameleonlike, it was transformed into its varicolored allotropes. Before the dawn of the Space Age, no one had ever imagined that such a world existed. Fascinating though it was to observe it from his comfortable vantage point, Poole found it hard to believe that men had ever risked landing there, where even robots feared to tread . . .

His main interest, however, was Europa, which at its closest appeared almost exactly the same size as Earth's solitary Moon, but raced through its phases in only four days. Though Poole had been quite unconscious of the symbolism when he chose his private landscape, it now seemed wholly appropriate that Europa should hang in the sky above another great enigma—the Sphinx.

Even with no magnification, when he requested the naked-eye view, Poole could see how greatly Europa had changed in the thousand years since *Discovery* had set out for Jupiter. The spider's web of narrow bands and lines that had once completely enveloped the smallest of the four Galilean satellites had vanished, except around the poles. Here the global crust of kilometer-thick ice remained unmelted by the warmth of Europa's new sun: elsewhere, virgin oceans seethed and boiled in the thin atmosphere, at what would have been comfortable room temperature on Earth.

It was also a comfortable temperature to the creatures who had emerged, after the melting of the unbroken ice shield that had both trapped and protected them. Orbiting spysats, showing details only centimeters across, had watched one Europan species starting to evolve into an amphibious stage: though they still spent much of their time underwater, the "Europs" had even begun the construction of simple buildings.

That this could happen in a mere thousand years was astonishing, but no one doubted that the explanation lay in the last and greatest of the Monoliths—the many-kilometers long "Great Wall" standing on the shore of the Sea of Galilee.

And no one doubted that, in its own mysterious way, it was watching over the experiment it had started on this world—as it had done on Earth four million years before.

19. THE MADNESS OF MANKIND

MISS PRINGLE

FILE—INDRA

My dear Indra—sorry I've not even voice-mailed you before—usual excuse, of course, so I won't bother to give it.

To answer your question—yes, I'm now feeling quite at home at the Grannymede, but am spending less and less time there, though I've been enjoying the sky display I've had piped into my suite. Last night the Io flux-tube put on a fine performance—that's a kind of lightning discharge between Io and Jupiter—I mean Lucifer. Rather like Earth's aurora, but much more spectacular. Discovered by the radio astronomers even before I was born.

And talking about ancient times—did you know that Anubis has a Sheriff? I think that's overdoing the frontier spirit. Reminds me of the stories my grandfather used to tell me about Arizona . . . Must try some of them on the Medes . . .

This may sound silly—I'm still not used to being in the Bowman Suite. I keep looking over my shoulder . . .

How do I spend my time? Much the same as in Africa Tower. I'm meeting the local intelligentsia, though as you might expect they're rather thin on the ground (hope no one is bugging this). And I've interacted—real and virtual—with the educational system—very good, it seems, though more technically oriented than you'd approve. That's inevitable, of course, in this hostile environment . . .

But it's helped me to understand why people live here. There's a challenge—a sense of purpose, if you like—that I seldom found on Earth.

It's true that most of the Medes were born here, so don't know any other home. Though they're—usually—too polite to say so, they think that the Home Planet is becoming decadent. Are you? And if so, what are you Terries—as the locals call you—going to do about it? One of the teenage classes I've met hopes to wake you up. They're drawing up elaborate Top Secret plans for the Invasion of Earth. Don't say I didn't warn you . . .

I've made one trip outside Anubis, into the so-called Night Land, where they never see Lucifer. Ten of us—Chandler, two of *Goliath*'s crew, six Medes—went into Farside, and chased the Sun down to the horizon so it really was night. Awesome—much like polar winters on Earth, but with the sky completely black . . . almost felt I was in space.

We could see all the Galileans beautifully, and watched Europa eclipse—sorry, occult—Io. Of course, the trip had been timed so we could observe this . . .

Several of the smaller satellites were just also visible, but the double star Earth–Moon was much more conspicuous. Did I feel homesick? Frankly, no—though I miss my new friends back there . . .

And I'm sorry—I still haven't met Dr. Khan, though he's left several messages for me. I promise to do it in the next few days—Earth days, not Mede ones!

Best wishes to Joe—regards to Danil, if you know what's happened to him—is he a real person again?—and my love to yourself . . .

STORE

TRANSMIT

Back in Poole's century, a person's name often gave a clue to his/her appearance, but that was no longer true thirty generations later. Dr. Theodore Khan turned out to be a Nordic blond who might have looked more at home in a Viking longboat than ravaging the steppes of Central Asia; however, he would not have been too impressive in either role, being less than a hundred and fifty centimeters tall. Poole could not resist a little amateur psychoanalysis: small people were often aggressive overachievers—which, from Indra Wallace's hints, appeared to be a good description of Ganymede's sole resident philosopher. Khan probably needed these qualifications to survive in such a practical-minded society.

Anubis City was far too small to boast a University campus—a luxury that still existed on the other worlds, though many believed that the telecommunications revolution had made it obsolete. Instead, it had something much more appropriate, as well as centuries older: an Academy, complete with a grove of olive trees that would have fooled Plato himself, until he had attempted to walk through it. Indra's joke about departments of philosophy requiring no more equipment than blackboards clearly did not apply in this sophisticated environment.

"It's built to hold seven people," said Dr. Khan proudly, when they had settled down on chairs obviously designed to be not-too-comfortable, "because that's the maximum one can efficiently interact with. And, if you count the ghost of Socrates, it was the number present when Phaedo delivered his famous address . . ."

"The one on the immortality of the soul?"

Khan was so obviously surprised that Poole could not help laughing.

"I took a crash course in philosophy just before I graduated—when the syllabus was planned, someone decided that we hairy-knuckled engineers should be exposed to a little culture."

"I'm delighted to hear it. That makes things so much easier. You know, I still can't credit my luck. Your arrival here almost tempts me to believe in miracles! I'd even thought of going to Earth to meet you—has dear Indra told you about my—ah—obsession?"

"No," Poole answered, not altogether truthfully.

Dr. Khan looked very pleased; he was clearly delighted to find a new audience.

"You may have heard me called an atheist, but that's not quite true. Atheism is unprovable, so uninteresting. However unlikely it is, we can never be certain that God once existed—and has now shot off to infinity, where no one can ever find him . . . Like Gautama Buddha, I take no position on this subject. My field of interest is the psychopathology known as Religion."

"Psychopathology? That's a harsh judgment."

"Amply justified by history. Imagine that you're an intelligent extraterrestrial, concerned only with verifiable truths. You discover a species that has divided itself into thousands—no, by now millions—of tribal groups holding an incredible variety of beliefs about the origin of the universe and the way to behave in it. Although many of them have ideas in common, even when there's a ninety-nine percent overlap, the remaining one percent's enough to set them killing and torturing each other, over trivial points of doctrine, utterly meaningless to outsiders.

"How to account for such irrational behavior? Lucretius hit it on the nail when he said that religion was the by-product of fear—a reaction to a mysterious and often hostile universe. For much of human prehistory, it may have been a necessary evil—but why was it so much more evil than necessary—and why did it survive when it was no longer necessary?

"I said evil—and I mean it, because fear leads to cruelty. The slightest knowledge of the Inquisition makes one ashamed to belong to the human species . . . One of the most revolting books ever published was the *Hammer of Witches*, written by a couple of sadistic perverts and describing the tortures the Church authorized—encouraged!—to extract 'confessions' from thousands of harmless old women, before it burned them alive . . . The Pope himself wrote an approving foreword!

"But most of the other religions, with a few honorable exceptions, were just as bad as Christianity . . . Even in your century, little boys were kept chained and whipped until they'd memorized whole volumes of pious gibberish, and robbed of their childhood and manhood to become monks . . .

"Perhaps the most baffling aspect of the whole affair is how obvious madmen, century after century, would proclaim that they—and they alone!—had received messages from God. If all the messages had agreed, that would have settled the matter. But of course they were wildly discordant—which never prevented self-styled messiahs from gathering hundreds—sometimes millions—of adherents, who would fight to the death against equally deluded believers of a microscopically differing faith."

Poole thought it was about time he got a word in edgewise.

"You've reminded me of something that happened in my hometown when I was a kid. A holy man—quote, unquote—set up shop, claimed he could work miracles—and collected a crowd of devotees in next to no time. And they weren't ignorant or illiterate; often they came from the best families. Every Sunday I used to see expensive cars parked round his—ah—temple."

"The 'Rasputin Syndrome,' it's been called: there are millions of such cases, all through history, in every country. And about one time in a thousand the cult survives for a couple of generations. What happened in this case?"

"Well, the competition was very unhappy, and did its best to discredit him. Wish I could remember his name—he used a long Indian one—Swami something-or-other—but it turned out he came from Alabama. One of his tricks was to produce holy objects out of thin air, and hand them to his worshippers. As it happened, our local rabbi was an amateur conjurer, and gave public demonstrations showing exactly how it was done. Didn't make the slightest difference; the faithful said that their man's magic was real, and the rabbi was just jealous.

"At one time, I'm sorry to say, Mother took the rascal seriously—it was soon after Dad had run off, which may have had something to do with it—and dragged me to one of his sessions. I was only about ten, but I thought I'd never seen anyone so unpleasant-looking. He had a beard that could have held several bird's nests, and probably did."

"He sounds like the standard model. How long did he flourish?"

"Three or four years. And then he had to leave town in a hurry: he was caught running teenage orgies. Of course, he claimed he was using mystical soul-saving techniques. And you won't believe this—"

"Try me."

"Even then, lots of his dupes still had faith in him. Their god could do no wrong, so he must have been framed."

"Framed?"

"Sorry—convicted by faked evidence—sometimes used by the police to catch criminals, when all else fails."

"Hmm. Well, your swami was perfectly typical: I'm rather disappointed. But he does help to prove my case—that most of humanity has always been insane, at least some of the time."

"Rather an unrepresentative sample—one small Flagstaff suburb."

"True, but I could multiply it by thousands—not only in your century, but all down the ages. There's never been anything, however absurd, that myriads of people weren't prepared to believe, often so passionately that they'd fight to the death rather than abandon their illusions. To me, that's a good operational definition of insanity."

"Would you argue that anyone with strong religious beliefs was insane?"

"In a strictly technical sense, yes—if they really were sincere, and not hypocrites. As I suspect ninety percent were."

"I'm certain that Rabbi Berenstein was sincere—and he was one of the sanest men I ever knew, as well as one of the finest. And how do you account for this? The only real genius I ever met was Dr. Chandra, who led the HAL project. I once had to go into his office—there was no reply when I knocked, and I thought it was unoccupied.

"He was praying to a group of fantastic little bronze statues, draped with flowers. One of them looked like an elephant . . . another had more than the regular number of arms . . . I was quite embarrassed, but luckily he didn't hear me and I tiptoed out. Would you say he was insane?"

"You've chosen a bad example: genius often is! So let's say: not insane, but mentally impaired, owing to childhood conditioning. The Jesuits claimed: 'Give me a boy for six years, and he is mine for life.' If they'd got hold of little Chandra in time, he'd have been a devout Catholic—not a Hindu."

"Possibly. But I'm puzzled—why were you so anxious to meet me? I'm afraid I've never been a devout anything. What have I got to do with all this?"

Slowly, and with the obvious enjoyment of a man unburdening himself of a heavy, long-hoarded secret, Dr. Khan told him.

20. APOSTATE

Hello, Frank . . . So you've finally met Ted. Yes, you could call him a crank—if you define that as an enthusiast with no sense of humor. But cranks often get that way because they know a Big Truth—can you hear my capitals?—and no one will listen . . . I'm glad you did—and I suggest you take him quite seriously.

You said you were surprised to see a Pope's portrait prominently displayed in Ted's apartment. That would have been his hero, Pius XX—I'm sure I mentioned him to you. Look him up—he's usually called the Impius! It's a fascinating story, and exactly parallels something that happened just before you were born. You must know how Mikhail Gorbachev, the President of the Soviet Empire, brought about its dissolution at the end of the Twentieth Century, by exposing its crimes and excesses.

He didn't intend to go that far—he'd hoped to reform it, but that was no longer possible. We'll never know if Pius XX had the same idea, because he was assassinated by a demented cardinal soon after he'd horrified the world by releasing the secret files of the Inquisition . . .

The religious were still shaken by the discovery of TMA-0 only a few decades earlier—that had a great impact on Pius XX, and certainly influenced his actions . . .

But you still haven't told me how Ted, that old crypto-Deist, thinks you can help him in his search for God. I believe he's still mad at him for hiding so successfully. Better not say I told you that.

On second thought, why not?
Love—Indra.
STORE
TRANSMIT

MISS PRINGLE
RECORD
Hello—Indra—I've had another session with Dr. Ted, though I've still not told him just why you think he's angry with God!

But I've had some very interesting arguments—no, dialogues—with him, though he does most of the talking. Never thought I'd get into philosophy again after all these years of engineering. Perhaps I had to go through them first, to appreciate it. Wonder how he'd grade me as a student?

Yesterday I tried this line of approach, to see his reaction. Perhaps it's original, though I doubt it. Thought you'd like to hear it—will be interested in your comments. Here's our discussion—

MISS PRINGLE—COPY AUDIO 94.

"Surely, Ted, you can't deny that most of the greatest works of human art have been inspired by religious devotion. Doesn't that prove something?"

"Yes—but not in a way that will give much comfort to any believers! From time to time, people amuse themselves making lists of the Biggests and Greatests and Bests—I'm sure that was a popular entertainment in your day."

"It certainly was."

"Well, there have been some famous attempts to do this with the arts. Of course such lists can't establish absolute— eternal—values, but they're interesting and show how tastes change from age to age . . .

"The last list I saw—it was on the Earth Artnet only a few years ago—was divided into Architecture, Music, Visual Arts . . . I remember a few of the examples . . . the Parthenon, the Taj Mahal . . . Bach's Toccata and Fugue was first in music, followed by Verdi's *Requiem Mass*. In art—the Mona Lisa, of course. Then—not sure of the order—a group of Buddha statues somewhere in Ceylon, and the golden death mask of young King Tut.

"Even if I could remember all the others—which of

course I can't—it doesn't matter: the important thing is their cultural and religious backgrounds. Overall, no single religion dominated—except in music. And that could be due to a purely technological accident: the organ and the other preelectronic musical instruments were perfected in the Christianized West. It could have worked out quite differently . . . if, for example, the Greeks or the Chinese had regarded machines as something more than toys.

"But what really settles the argument, as far as I'm concerned, is the general consensus about the single greatest work of human art. Over and over again, in almost every listing—it's Angkor Wat. Yet the religion that inspired that has been extinct for centuries; no one even knows precisely what it was, except that it involved hundreds of gods, not merely one!"

"Wish I could have thrown that at dear old Rabbi Berenstein—I'm sure he'd have had a good answer."

"I don't doubt it. I wish I could have met him myself. And I'm glad he never lived to see what happened to Israel."

END AUDIO.

There you have it, Indra. Wish the Grannymede had Angkor Wat on its menu—I've never seen it—but you can't have everything . . .

Now, the question you really wanted answered . . . why is Dr. Ted so delighted that I'm here?

As you know, he's convinced that the key to many mysteries lies on Europa, where no one has been allowed to land for a thousand years.

He thinks I may be an exception. He believes I have a friend there. Yes—Dave Bowman, or whatever he's now become . . .

We know that he survived being drawn into the Big Brother Monolith—and somehow revisited Earth afterward. But there's more, that I didn't know. Very few people do, because the Medes are embarrassed to talk about it . . .

Ted Khan has spent years collecting the evidence, and is now quite certain of the facts—even though he can't explain them. On at least six occasions, about a century apart, reliable observers here in Anubis have reported seeing an—apparition—just like the one that Heywood Floyd met aboard *Discovery*. Though not one of them knew about that incident, they were all able to identify Dave when they were shown his hologram. And there was another sighting aboard a survey ship that made a close approach to Europa, six hundred years ago . . .

Individually, no one would take these cases seriously, but altogether they make a pattern. Ted's quite sure that Dave Bowman survives in some form, presumably associated with the Monolith we call the Great Wall. And he still has some interest in our affairs.

Though he's made no attempt at communication, Ted hopes we can make contact. He believes that I'm the only human who can do it . . .

I'm still trying to make up my mind. Tomorrow I'll talk it over with Captain Chandler. Will let you know what we decide. Love, Frank.

STORE

TRANSMIT—INDRA

21. QUARANTINE

"Do you believe in ghosts, Dim?"

"Certainly not: but like every sensible man, I'm afraid of them. Why do you ask?"

"If it wasn't a ghost, it was the most vivid dream I've ever had. Last night I had a conversation with Dave Bowman."

Poole knew that Captain Chandler would take him seriously, when the occasion required; nor was he disappointed.

"Interesting—but there's an obvious explanation. You've been living here in the Bowman Suite, for Deus' sake! You told me yourself it feels haunted."

"I'm sure—well, ninety-nine percent sure—that you're right, and the whole thing was prompted by the discussions I've been having with Proff Ted. Have you heard the reports that Dave Bowman occasionally appears in Anubis? About once every hundred years? Just as he did to Dr. Floyd aboard *Discovery*, after she'd been reactivated."

"What happened there? I've heard vague stories, but never taken them seriously."

"Dr. Khan does, and so do I—I've seen the original recordings. Floyd's sitting in my old chair when a kind of dust-cloud forms behind him, and shapes itself into Dave's head. Then it gives that famous message, warning him to leave."

"Who wouldn't? But that was a thousand years ago. Plenty of time to fake it."

"What would be the point? Khan and I were looking at it yesterday. I'd bet my life it's authentic."

"As a matter of fact, I agree with you. And I have heard those reports . . ."

Chandler's voice trailed away, and he looked slightly embarrassed. "Long time ago, I had a girlfriend here in Anubis. She told me that her grandfather had seen Bowman. I laughed."

"I wonder if Ted has that sighting on his list. Could you put him in touch with your friend?"

"Er—rather not. We haven't spoken for years. For all I know, she may be on the Moon, or Mars . . . Anyway, why is Professor Ted interested?"

"That's what I really wanted to discuss with you."

"Sounds ominous. Go ahead."

"Ted thinks that Dave Bowman, or whatever he's become, may still exist—up there on Europa."

"After a thousand years?"

"Well—look at me."

"One sample is poor statistics, my math prof used to say. But go on."

"It's a complicated story—or maybe a jigsaw, with most of the pieces missing. But it's generally agreed that something crucial happened to our ancestors when that Monolith appeared in Africa, four million years ago. It marks a turning point in prehistory—the first appearance of tools—and weapons—and religion . . . That can't be pure coincidence. The Monolith must have done something to us— surely it couldn't have just stood there, passively accepting worship . . .

"Ted's fond of quoting a famous paleontologist who said, 'TMA-0 gave us an evolutionary kick in the pants.' He argues that the kick wasn't in a wholly desirable direction. Did we have to become so mean and nasty to survive? Maybe we did . . . As I understand him, Ted believes that there's something fundamentally wrong with the wiring of our brains, which makes us incapable of consistent logical thinking. To make matters worse, though all creatures need a certain amount of aggressiveness to survive, we seem to have far more than is absolutely necessary. And no other animal tortures its fellows as we do. Is this an evolutionary accident—a piece of genetic bad luck?

"It's also widely agreed that TMA-1 was planted on the Moon to keep track of the project—experiment—whatever it was—and to report to Jupiter—the obvious place for Solar System Mission Control. That's why another Monolith—Big Brother—was waiting there. Had been waiting four million years, when *Discovery* arrived. Agreed so far?"

"Yes; I've always thought that was the most plausible theory."

"Now for the more speculative stuff. Bowman was apparently swallowed up by Big Brother, yet something of his personality seems to have survived. Twenty years after that encounter with Heywood Floyd in the second Jupiter expedition, they had another contact aboard *Universe*, when Floyd joined it for the 2061 rendezvous with Halley's Comet. At least, so he tells us in his memoirs—though he was well over a hundred when he dictated them."

"Could have been senile."

"Not according to all the contemporary accounts! Also—perhaps even more significant—his grandson Chris had some equally weird experiences when *Galaxy* made its forced landing on Europa. And, of course, that's where the Monolith—or a Monolith—is, right now! Surrounded by Europans . . ."

"I'm beginning to see what Dr. Ted's driving at. This is where we came in—the whole cycle's starting over again. The Europs are being groomed for stardom."

"Exactly—everything fits. Jupiter ignited to give them a sun, to thaw out their frozen world. The warning to us to keep our distance—presumably so that we wouldn't interfere with their development . . ."

"Where have I heard that idea before? Of course, Frank—it goes back a thousand years—to your own time! 'The Prime Directive'! We still get lots of laughs from those old *Star Trek* programs."

"Did I ever tell you I once met some of the actors? They would have been surprised to see me now . . . And I've always had two thoughts about that noninterference policy. The Monolith certainly violated it with us, back there in Africa. One might argue that did have disastrous results . . ."

"So better luck next time—on Europa!"

Poole laughed, without much humor.

"Khan used those exact words."

"And what does he think we should do about it? Above all—where do you come into the picture?"

"First of all, we must find out what's really happening on Europa—and why. Merely observing it from space is not enough."

"What else can we do? All the probes the Medes have sent there were blown up, just before landing."

"And ever since the mission to rescue *Galaxy*, crew-carrying ships have been diverted by some field of force, which no one can figure out. Very interesting: it proves that whatever is down there is protective, but not malevolent. And—this is the important point—it must have some way of scanning what's on the way. It can distinguish between robots and humans."

"More than I can do, sometimes. Go on."

"Well, Ted thinks there's one human being who might make it down to the surface of Europa—because his old friend is there, and may have some influence with the powers-that-be."

Captain Dimitri Chandler gave a long, low whistle.

"And you're willing to risk it?"

"Yes: what have I got to lose?"

"One valuable shuttle craft, if I know what you have in mind. Is that why you've been learning to fly *Falcon*?"

"Well, now that you mention it . . . the idea had occurred to me."

"I'll have to think it over—I'll admit I'm intrigued, but there are lots of problems."

"Knowing you, I'm sure they won't stand in the way—once you've decided to help me."

22. VENTURE

MISS PRINGLE—LIST PRIORITY MESSAGES FROM EARTH
RECORD

Dear Indra—I'm not trying to be dramatic, but this may be my last message from Ganymede. By the time you receive it, I will be on my way to Europa.

Though it's a sudden decision—and no one is more surprised than I am—I've thought it over very carefully. As you'll have guessed, Ted Khan is largely responsible . . . let him do the explaining, if I don't come back.

Please don't misunderstand me—in no way do I regard this as a suicide mission! But I'm ninety percent convinced by Ted's arguments, and he's aroused my curiosity so much that I'd never forgive myself if I turned down this once in a lifetime opportunity. Maybe I should say once in two lifetimes . . .

I'm flying *Goliath*'s little one-person shuttle, *Falcon*—how I'd have loved to demonstrate her to my old colleagues back at the Space Administration! Judging by past records, the most likely outcome is that I'll be diverted from Europa before I can land. Even this will teach me something . . .

And if it—presumably the local Monolith, the Great Wall—decides to treat me like the robot probes it's zapped in the past, I'll never know. That's a risk I'm prepared to take.

Thank you for everything, and my very best to Joe. Love from Ganymede—and soon, I hope, from Europa.

STORE
TRANSMIT

IV. THE KINGDOM
OF SULFUR

23. FALCON

"Europa's about four hundred thousand kay from Ganymede at the moment," Captain Chandler informed Poole. "If you stepped on the gas—thanks for teaching me that phrase!—*Falcon* could get you there in an hour. But I wouldn't recommend it: our mysterious friend might be alarmed by anyone coming in that fast."

"Agreed—and I want time to think. I'm going to take several hours, at least. And I'm still hoping . . ." Poole's voice trailed off into silence.

"Hoping what?"

"That I can make some sort of contact with Dave, or whatever it is, before I attempt to land."

"Yes, it's always rude to drop in uninvited—even with people you know, let alone perfect strangers like the Europs. Perhaps you should take some gifts—what did the old-time explorers use? I believe mirrors and beads were once popular."

Chandler's facetious tone did not disguise his real concern, both for Poole and for the valuable piece of equipment he proposed to borrow—and for which the skipper of *Goliath* was ultimately responsible.

"I'm still trying to decide how we work this. If you come back a hero, I want to bask in your reflected glory. But if you lose *Falcon* as well as yourself, what shall I say? That you stole the shuttle while we weren't looking? I'm afraid no one would buy that story. Ganymede Traffic Control's very efficient—has to be! If you left without advance notice, they'd be on to you in a microsec—well, a millisecond. No way you could leave unless I file your flight plan ahead of time.

"So this is what I propose to do, unless I think of something better.

"You're taking *Falcon* out for a final qualification test—everyone knows you've already soloed. You'll go into a two-thousand-kilometer-high orbit above Europa—nothing unusual about that—people do it all the time, and the local authorities don't seem to object.

"Estimated total flight time five hours plus or minus ten minutes. If you suddenly change your mind about coming home, no one can do anything about it—at least, no one on Ganymede. Of course, I'll make some indignant noises, and say how astonished I am by such gross navigational errors, etc., etc. Whatever will look best in the subsequent Court of Enquiry."

"Would it come to that? I don't want to do anything that will get you into trouble."

"Don't worry—it's time there was a little excitement round here. But only you and I know about this plot; try not to mention it to the crew—I want them to have—what was that other useful expression you taught me?—'plausible deniability.' "

"Thanks, Dim—I really appreciate what you're doing. And I hope you'll never have to regret hauling me aboard *Goliath*, out round Neptune."

Poole found it hard to avoid arousing suspicion, by the way he behaved toward his new crewmates as they prepared *Falcon* for what was supposed to be a short, routine flight. Only he and Chandler knew that it might be nothing of the kind.

Yet he was not heading into the totally unknown, as he and Dave Bowman had done a thousand years ago. Stored in the shuttle's memory were high-resolution maps of Europa showing details down to a few meters across. He knew exactly where he wished to go; it only remained to see if he would be allowed to break the centuries-long quarantine.

24. ESCAPE

"Manual control, please."

"Are you sure, Frank?"

"Quite sure, *Falcon* . . . Thank you."

Illogical though it seemed, most of the human race had found it impossible not to be polite to its artificial children, however simpleminded they might be. Whole volumes of psychology, as well as popular guides (*How Not to Hurt Your Computer's Feelings; Artificial Intelligence—Real Irritation* were some of the best-known titles) had been written on the subject of Man-Machine etiquette. Long ago it had been decided that, however inconsequential rudeness to robots might appear to be, it should be discouraged. All too easily, it could spread to human relationships as well.

Falcon was now in orbit, just as her flight plan had promised, at a safe two thousand kilometers above Europa. The giant moon's crescent dominated the sky ahead, and even the area not illuminated by Lucifer was so brilliantly lit by the much more distant sun that every detail was clearly visible. Poole needed no optical aid to see his planned destination, on the still icy shore of the Sea of Galilee, not far from the skeleton of the first spacecraft to land on this world. Though the Europans had long ago removed all its metal components, the ill-fated Chinese ship still served as a memorial to its crew; and it was appropriate that the only "town"—even if an alien one—on this whole world should have been named "Tsienville."

Poole had decided to come down over the Sea, and then fly very slowly toward Tsienville—hoping that this approach would appear friendly, or at least nonaggressive. Though he admitted to himself that this was very naive, he could think of no better alternative.

Then, suddenly, just as he was dropping below the thousand-kilometer level, there was an interruption—not of the kind he had hoped for, but one that he had been expecting.

"This is Ganymede Control calling *Falcon*. You have departed from your flight plan. Please advise immediately what is happening."

It was hard to ignore such an urgent request, but in the circumstances it seemed the best thing to do.

Exactly thirty seconds later, and a hundred kilometers closer to Europa, Ganymede repeated its message. Once again Poole ignored it—but *Falcon* did not.

"Are you quite sure you want to do this, Frank?" asked the shuttle. Though Poole knew perfectly well that he was imagining it, he would have sworn there was a note of anxiety in its voice.

"Quite sure, *Falcon*. I know exactly what I'm doing."

That was certainly untrue, and any moment now further lying might be necessary, to a more sophisticated audience.

Seldom-activated indicator lights started to flash near the edge of the control board. Poole smiled with satisfaction: everything was going according to plan.

"This is Ganymede Control! Do you receive me, *Falcon*? You are operating on manual override, so I am unable to assist you. What is happening? You are still descending toward Europa. Please acknowledge immediately."

Poole began to experience mild twinges of conscience. He thought he recognized the Controller's voice, and was almost certain that it was a charming lady he had met at a reception given by the Mayor, soon after his arrival at Anubis. She sounded genuinely alarmed.

Suddenly, he knew how to relieve her anxiety—as well as to attempt something that he had previously dismissed as altogether too absurd. Perhaps, after all, it was worth a try: it certainly wouldn't do any harm—and it might even work.

"This is Frank Poole, calling from *Falcon*. I am perfectly O.K.—but something seems to have taken over the controls, and is bringing the shuttle down toward Europa. I hope you are receiving this—I will continue to report as long as possible."

Well, he hadn't actually lied to the worried Controller, and one day he hoped he would be able to face her with a clear conscience.

He continued to talk, trying to sound as if he was completely sincere, instead of skirting the edge of truth.

"I repeat, this is Frank Poole aboard the shuttle *Falcon*, descending toward Europa. I assume that some outside force has taken charge of my spacecraft, and will be landing it safely.

"Dave—this is your old shipmate Frank. Are you the entity that is controlling me? I have reason to think that you are on Europa.

"If so—I look forward to meeting you—wherever or whatever you are."

Not for a moment did he imagine there would be any reply: even Ganymede Control appeared to be shocked into silence.

And yet, in a way, he had an answer. *Falcon* was still being permitted to descend toward the Sea of Galilee.

Europa was only fifty kilometers below; with his naked eyes Poole could now see the narrow black bar where the greatest of the Monoliths stood guard—if indeed it was doing that—on the outskirts of Tsienville.

No human being had been allowed to come so close for a thousand years.

25. FIRE IN THE DEEP

For millions of years it had been an ocean world, its hidden waters protected from the vacuum of space by a crust of ice. In most places the ice was kilometers thick, but there were lines of weakness where it had cracked open and torn apart. Then there had been a brief battle between two implacably hostile elements that came into direct contact on no other world in the Solar System. The war between Sea and Space always ended in the same stalemate; the exposed water simultaneously boiled and froze, repairing the armor of ice.

The seas of Europa would have frozen completely solid long ago without the influence of nearby Jupiter. Its gravity continually kneaded the core of the little world; the forces that convulsed Io were also working there, though with much less ferocity. Everywhere in the deep was evidence of that tug-of-war between planet and satellite, in the continual roar and thunder of submarine earthquakes, the shriek of gases escaping from the interior, the infrasonic pressure waves of avalanches sweeping over the abyssal plains. By comparison with the tumultuous ocean that covered Europa, even the noisy seas of Earth were silent.

Here and there, scattered over the deserts of the deep, were oases that would have amazed and delighted any terrestrial biologist. They extended for several kilometers around tangled masses of pipes and chimneys deposited by mineral brines gushing from the interior. Often they created natural parodies of Gothic castles, from which black, scalding liquids pulsed in a slow rhythm, as if driven by the beating of some mighty heart. And like blood, they were the authentic sign of life itself.

The boiling fluids drove back the deadly cold leaking down from above, and formed islands of warmth on the seabed. Equally important, they brought from Europa's interior all the chemicals of life. Such fertile oases, offering food and energy in abundance, had been discovered by the Twentieth-Century explorers of Earth's oceans. Here they were present on an immensely larger scale, and in far greater variety.

Delicate, spidery structures that seemed to be the analog of plants flourished in the "tropical" zones closest to the sources of heat. Crawling among these were bizarre slugs and worms, some feeding on the plants, others obtaining their food directly from the mineral-laden waters around them. At greater distances from the submarine fires around which all these creatures warmed themselves lived sturdier, more robust organisms, not unlike crabs or spiders.

Armies of biologists could have spent lifetimes studying one small oasis. Unlike the Paleozoic terrestrial seas, the Europan abyss was not a stable environment, so evolution had progressed with astonishing speed, producing multitudes of fantastic forms. And all were under the same indefinite stay of execution; sooner or later, each fountain of life would weaken and die, as the forces that powered it moved their focus elsewhere. All across the Europan seabed was evidence of such tragedies; countless circular areas were littered with the skeletons and mineral-encrusted remains of dead creatures, where entire chapters of evolution had been deleted from the book of life. Some had left as their only memorial huge, empty shells like convoluted trumpets, larger than a man. And there were clams of many shapes—bivalves, and even trivalves, as well as spiral stone patterns, many meters across—exactly like the beautiful ammonites that disappeared so mysteriously from Earth's oceans at the end of the Cretaceous Period.

Among the greatest wonders of the Europan abyss were rivers of incandescent lava, pouring from the calderas of submarine volcanoes. The pressure at these depths was so great that the water in contact with the red-hot magma could not flash into steam, so the two liquids coexisted in an uneasy truce.

There, on another world and with alien actors, something like the story of Egypt had been played out long before the coming of Man. As the Nile had brought life to a narrow ribbon of desert, so this river of warmth had vivified the Europan deep. Along its banks, in a band never more than a few kilometers wide, species after species had evolved and flourished and passed away. And some had left permanent monuments.

Often, they were not easy to distinguish from the natural formations around the thermal vents, and even when they were clearly not due to pure chemistry, one would be hard put to decide whether they were the product of instinct or intelligence. On Earth, the termites reared condominiums almost as impressive as any found in the single vast ocean that enveloped this frozen world.

Along the narrow band of fertility in the deserts of the deep, whole cultures and even civilizations might have risen and fallen, armies might have marched—or swum—under the command of Europan Tamerlanes or Napoleons. And the rest of their world would never have known, for all their oases were as isolated from one another as the planets themselves. The creatures who basked in the glow of the lava rivers, and fed around the hot vents, could not cross the hostile wilderness between their lonely islands. If they had ever produced historians and philosophers, each culture would have been convinced that it was alone in the Universe.

Yet even the space between the oases was not altogether empty of life; there were hardier creatures who had dared its rigors. Some were the Europan analogs of fish—streamlined torpedoes, propelled by vertical tails, steered by fins along their bodies. The resemblance to the most successful dwellers in Earth's oceans was inevitable; given the same engineering problems, evolution must produce very similar answers. Witness the dolphin and the shark—superficially almost identical, yet from far distant branches of the tree of life.

There was, however, one very obvious difference between the fish of the Europan seas and those in terrestrial oceans; they had no gills, for there was hardly a trace of oxygen to be extracted from the waters in which they swam. Like the creatures around Earth's own geothermal vents, their metabolism was based on sulfur compounds, present in abundance in this volcanic environment.

And very few had eyes. Apart from the flickering glow of lava outpourings, and occasional bursts of bioluminescence from creatures seeking mates, or hunters questing for prey, it was a lightless world.

It was also a doomed one. Not only were its energy sources sporadic and constantly shifting, but the tidal forces that drove them were steadily weakening. Even if they developed true intelligence, the Europans were trapped between fire and ice.

Barring a miracle, they would perish with the final freezing of their little world.

Lucifer had wrought that miracle.

26. TSIENVILLE

In the final moments, as he came in over the coast at a sedate hundred kilometers an hour, Poole wondered if there might be some last-minute intervention. But nothing untoward happened, even when he moved slowly along the black, forbidding face of the Great Wall.

It was the inevitable name for the Europa Monolith, as, unlike its little brothers on Earth and the Moon, it was lying horizontally, and was more than twenty kilometers long. Although it was literally billions of times greater in volume than TMA-0 and TMA-1, its proportions were exactly the same—that intriguing ratio 1:4:9, inspirer of so much numeralogical nonsense over the centuries.

As the vertical face was almost ten kilometers high, one plausible theory maintained that among its other functions the Great Wall served as a windbreak, protecting Tsienville from the ferocious gales that occasionally roared in from the Sea of Galilee. They were much less frequent now that the climate had stabilized, but a thousand years earlier they would have been a severe discouragement to any life-forms emerging from the ocean.

Though he had fully intended to do so, Poole had never found time to visit the Tycho Monolith—still Top Secret when he had left for Jupiter—and Earth's gravity made its twin at Olduvai inaccessible to him. But he had seen their images so often that they were much more familiar than the proverbial back of the hand (and how many people, he had often wondered, would recognize the backs of their hands?). Apart from the enormous difference in scale, there was absolutely no way of distinguishing the Great Wall from TMA-1 and TMA-0—or, for that matter, the "Big Brother" that *Leonov* had encountered orbiting Jupiter.

According to some theories, perhaps crazy enough to be true, there was only one archetypal Monolith, and all the others—whatever their size—were merely projections or images of it. Poole recalled these ideas when he noticed the spotless, unsullied smoothness of the Great Wall's towering ebon face. Surely, after so many centuries in such a hostile environment, it should have collected a few patches of grime! Yet it looked as immaculate as if an army of window cleaners had just polished every square centimeter.

Then he recalled that although everyone who had ever come to view TMA-1 and TMA-0 felt an irresistible urge to touch their apparently pristine surfaces, no one had ever succeeded. Fingers, diamond drills, laser knives—all skittered across the Monoliths as if they were coated by an impenetrable film. Or as if—and this was another popular theory—they were not quite in this universe, but somehow separated from it by an utterly impassable fraction of a millimeter.

He made one complete, leisurely circuit of the Great Wall, which remained totally indifferent to his progress. Then he brought the shuttle—still on manual, in case Ganymede Control made any further attempts to "rescue" him—to the outer limits of Tsienville, and hovered there looking for the best place to land.

The scene through *Falcon*'s small panoramic window was wholly familiar to him; he had examined it so often in Ganymede recordings, never imagining that one day he would be observing it in reality. The Europs, it seemed, had no idea of town planning; hundreds of hemispherical structures were scattered apparently at random over an area about a kilometer across. Some were so small that even human children would feel cramped in them; though others were big enough to hold a large family, none was more than five meters high.

And they were all made from the same material, which gleamed a ghostly white in the double daylight. On Earth, the Eskimos had found the identical answer to the challenge of their own frigid, materials-poor environment; Tsienville's igloos were also made of ice.

In lieu of streets, there were canals—as best suited creatures who were still partly amphibious, and apparently returned to the water to sleep. Also, it was believed, to feed and to mate, though neither hypothesis had been proved.

Tsienville had been called "Venice, made of ice," and Poole had to agree that it was an apt description. However, there were no Venetians in sight; the place looked as if it had been deserted for years.

And here was another mystery: despite the fact that Lucifer was fifty times brighter than the distant Sun, and was a permanent fixture in the sky, the Europs still seemed locked to an ancient rhythm of night and day. They returned to the ocean at sunset, and emerged with the rising of the Sun—despite the fact that the level of illumination had changed by only a few percent. Perhaps there was a parallel on Earth, where the life cycles of many creatures were controlled as much by the feeble Moon as the far more brilliant Sun.

It would be sunrise in another hour, and then the inhabitants of Tsienville would return to land and go about their leisurely affairs—as by human standards, they certainly were. The sulfur-based biochemistry that powered the Europs was not as efficient as the oxygen-driven one that energized the vast majority of terrestrial animals. Even a sloth could outrun a Europ, so it was difficult to regard them as potentially dangerous. That was the Good News; the Bad News was that even with the best intentions on both sides, attempts at communication would be extremely slow—perhaps intolerably tedious.

It was about time, Poole decided, that he reported back to Ganymede Control. They must be getting very anxious, and he wondered how his co-conspirator, Captain Chandler, was dealing with the situation.

"*Falcon* calling Ganymede. As you can doubtless see, I have—er—been brought to rest just above Tsienville. There is no sign of hostility, and as it's still solar night here all the Europs are underwater. Will call you again as soon as I'm on the ground."

Dim would have been proud of him, Poole thought, as he brought *Falcon* down gently as a snowflake on a smooth patch of ice. He was taking no chances with its stability, and set the inertial drive to cancel all but a fraction of the shuttle's weight—just enough, he hoped, to prevent its being blown away by any wind.

He was on Europa—the first human in a thousand years. Had Armstrong and Aldrin felt this sense of elation, when the *Eagle* touched down on the Moon? Probably they were too busy checking their Lunar Module's primitive and totally unintelligent systems.

Falcon, of course, was doing all this automatically. The little cabin was now very quiet, apart from the inevitable—and reassuring—murmur of well-tempered electronics. It gave Poole a considerable shock when Chandler's voice, obviously prerecorded, interrupted his thoughts.

"So you made it! Congratulations! As you know, we're scheduled to return to the Belt week after next, but that should give you plenty of time.

"After five days, *Falcon* knows what to do. She'll find her way home, with or without you. So good luck!"

MISS PRINGLE

ACTIVATE CRYPTO PROGRAM

STORE

Hello, Dim—thanks for that cheerful message! I feel rather silly using this program—as if I'm a secret agent in one of the spy melodramas that used to be so popular before I was born. Still, it will allow some privacy, which may be useful. Hope Miss Pringle has downloaded it properly . . . of course, Miss P., I'm only joking!

By the way, I'm getting a barrage of requests from all the news media in the Solar System. Please try to hold them off—or divert them to Dr. Ted. He'll enjoy handling them . . .

Since Ganymede has me on camera all the time, I won't waste breath telling you what I'm seeing. If all goes well, we should have some action in a few minutes—and we'll know if it really was a good idea, to let the Europs find me already sitting here peacefully, waiting to greet them when they come to the surface . . .

Whatever happens, it won't be as big a surprise to me as it was to Dr. Chang and his colleagues, when they landed here a thousand years ago! I played his famous last message again, just before leaving Ganymede. I must confess it gave me an eerie feeling—couldn't help wondering if something like that could possibly happen again . . . wouldn't like to immortalize myself the way poor Chang did . . .

Of course, I can always lift off if something starts going wrong . . . and here's an interesting thought that's just occurred to me . . . I wonder if the Europs have any history—any kind of records . . . any memory of what happened just a few kilometers from here, a thousand years ago?

27. ICE AND VACUUM

"... This is Dr. Chang, calling from Europa, I hope you can hear me, especially Dr. Floyd—I know you are aboard *Leonov* . . . I may not have much time . . . aiming my suit antenna where I think you are . . . please relay this information to Earth.

"*Tsien* was destroyed three hours ago. I'm the only survivor. Using my suit radio—no idea if it has enough range, but it's the only chance. Please listen carefully . . .

"THERE IS LIFE ON EUROPA. I repeat: THERE IS LIFE ON EUROPA . . .

"We landed safely, checked all the systems, and ran out the hoses so we could start pumping water into our propellant tanks immediately . . . just in case we had to leave in a hurry.

"Everything was going according to plan . . . it seemed almost too good to be true. The tanks were half full when Dr. Lee and I went out to check the pipe insulation. *Tsien* stands—stood—about thirty meters from the edge of the Grand Canal. Pipes went directly from it and down through the ice. Very thin—not safe to walk on.

"Jupiter was quarter full, and we had five kilowatts of lighting strung up on the ship. She looked like a Christmas tree—beautiful, reflected on the ice . . .

"Lee saw it first—a huge dark mass rising up from the depths. At first we thought it was a school of fish—too large for a single organism—then it started to break through the ice, and began moving toward us.

"It looked rather like huge strands of wet seaweed, crawling along the ground. Lee ran back to the ship to get a camera—I stayed to watch, reporting over the radio. The thing moved so slowly I could easily outrun it. I was much more excited than alarmed. Thought I knew what kind of creature it was—I've seen pictures of the kelp forests off California—but I was quite wrong.

". . . I could tell it was in trouble. It couldn't possibly survive at a temperature a hundred and fifty below its normal environment. It was freezing solid as it moved forward—bits were breaking off like glass—but it was still advancing toward the ship, a black tidal wave, slowing down all the time.

"I was still so surprised that I couldn't think straight and I couldn't imagine what it was trying to do. Even though it was heading toward *Tsien* it still seemed completely harmless, like—well, a small forest on the move. I remember smiling—it reminded me of Macbeth's Burnham Wood . . .

"Then I suddenly realized the danger. Even if it was completely inoffensive—it was heavy—with all the ice it was carrying, it must have weighed several tons, even in this low gravity. And it was slowly, painfully climbing up our landing gear . . . the legs were beginning to buckle, all in slow motion, like something in a dream—or a nightmare . . .

"Not until the ship started to topple did I realize what the thing was trying to do—and then it was far too late. We could have saved ourselves—if we'd only switched off our lights!

"Perhaps it's a phototrope, its biological cycle triggered by the sunlight that filters down through the ice. Or it could have been attracted like a moth to a candle. Our floodlights must have been more brilliant than anything Europa has ever known, even the sun itself . . .

"Then the ship crashed. I saw the hull split, a cloud of snowflakes form as moisture condensed. All the lights went out, except for one, swinging back and forth on a cable a couple of meters above the ground.

"I don't know what happened immediately after that. The next thing I remember, I was standing under the light, beside the wreck of the ship, with a fine powdering of fresh snow all around me. I could see my footsteps in it very clearly. I must have run there; perhaps only a minute or two had elapsed . . .

"The plant—I still thought of it as a plant—was motionless. I wondered if it had been damaged by the impact; large sections—as thick as a man's arm—had splintered off, like broken twigs.

"Then the main trunk started to move again. It pulled away from the hull, and began to crawl toward me. That was when I knew for certain that the thing was light-sensitive: I was standing immediately under the thousand-watt lamp, which had stopped swinging now.

"Imagine an oak tree—better still, a banyan with its multiple trunks and roots—flattened out by gravity and trying to creep along the ground. It got to within five meters of the light, then started to spread out until it had made a perfect circle around me. Presumably that was the limit of its tolerance—the point at which photoattraction turned to repulsion.

"After that, nothing happened for several minutes. I wondered if it was dead—frozen solid at last.

"Then I saw that large buds were forming on many of the branches. It was like watching a time-lapse film of flowers opening. In fact I thought they were flowers—each about as big as a man's head.

"Delicate, beautifully colored membranes started to unfold. Even then, it occurred to me that no one—no *thing*—could ever have seen these colors properly, until we brought our lights—our fatal lights—to this world.

"Tendrils, stamens, waving feebly . . . I walked over to the living wall that surrounded me, so that I could see exactly what was happening. Neither then, nor at any other time, had I felt the slightest fear of the creature. I was certain that it was not malevolent—if indeed it was conscious at all.

"There were scores of the big flowers, in various stages of unfolding. Now they reminded me of butterflies, just emerging from the chrysalis—wings crumpled, still feeble—I was getting closer and closer to the truth.

"But they were freezing—dying as quickly as they formed. Then, one after another, they dropped off from the parent buds. For a few moments they flopped around like fish stranded on dry land—and at last I realized exactly what they were. Those membranes weren't petals—they were *fins*, or their equivalent. This was the free-swimming larval stage of the creature. Probably it spends much of its life rooted on the seabed, then sends these mobile offspring in search of new territory. Just like the corals of Earth's oceans.

"I knelt down to get a closer look at one of the little creatures. The beautiful colors were fading now, to a drab brown. Some of the petal-fins had snapped off, becoming brittle shards as they froze. But it was still moving feebly, and as I approached it tried to avoid me. I wondered how it sensed my presence.

"Then I noticed that the *stamens*—as I'd called them—all carried bright blue dots at their tips. They looked like tiny star sapphires—or the blue eyes along the mantle of a scallop—aware of light, but unable to form true images. As I watched, the vivid blue faded, the gems became dull, ordinary stones . . .

"Dr. Floyd—or anyone else who is listening—I haven't much more time; my life-support system alarm has just sounded. But I've almost finished.

"I knew then what I had to do. The cable to that thousand-watt lamp was hanging almost to the ground. I gave it a few tugs, and the light went out in a shower of sparks.

"I wondered whether it was too late. For a few minutes nothing happened. So I walked over to the wall of tangled branches around me, and *kicked* it.

"Slowly, the creature started to unweave itself, and to retreat back to the Canal. I followed it all the way back to the water, encouraging it with more kicks when it slowed down, feeling the fragments of ice crunching all the time beneath my boots . . . As it neared the Canal, it seemed to gain strength and energy, as if it knew it was approaching its natural home. I wondered if it would survive, to bud again.

"It disappeared through the surface, leaving a few last dead larvae on the alien land. The exposed free water bubbled for a few minutes until a scab of protective ice sealed it from the vacuum above. Then I walked back to the ship to see if there was anything to salvage—I don't want to talk about that.

"I've only two requests to make, Doctor. When the taxonomists classify this creature, I hope they'll name it after me.

"And—when the next ship comes home—ask them to take our bones back to China.

"I'll lose power in a few minutes—wish I knew whether anyone was receiving me. Anyway, I'll repeat this message as long as I can . . .

"This is Professor Chang on Europa, reporting the destruction of the spaceship *Tsien*. We landed beside the Grand Canal and set up our pumps at the edge of the ice—"

28. THE LITTLE DAWN

MISS PRINGLE
RECORD
Here comes the Sun! Strange—how quickly it seems to rise, on this slowly turning world! Of course, of course—the disk's so small that the whole of it pops above the horizon in no time . . . Not that it makes much difference to the light—if you weren't looking in that direction, you'd never notice that there was another sun in the sky.

But I hope the Europs have noticed. Usually it takes them less than five minutes to start coming ashore after the Little Dawn. Wonder if they already know I'm here, and are scared . . .

No—could be the other way round. Perhaps they're inquisitive—even anxious to see what strange visitor has come to Tsienville . . . I rather hope so . . .

Here they come! Hope your spysats are watching—*Falcon*'s cameras recording . . .

How slowly they move! I'm afraid it's going to be very boring trying to communicate with them . . . even if they want to talk to me . . .

Rather like the thing that overturned *Tsien*, but much smaller . . . They remind me of little trees, walking on half a dozen slender trunks. And with hundreds of branches, dividing into twigs, which divide again . . . and again. Just like many of our general-purpose robots . . . what a long time it took us to realize that imitation humanoids were ridiculously clumsy, and the proper way to go was with myriads of small manipulators! Whenever we invent something clever, we find that Mother Nature's already thought of it . . .

Aren't the little ones cute—like tiny bushes on the move. Wonder how they reproduce—budding? I hadn't realized how beautiful they are. Almost as colorful as coral reef fish—maybe for the same reasons . . . to attract mates, or fool predators by pretending to be something else . . .

Did I say they looked like bushes? Make that rosebushes—they've actually got thorns! Must have a good reason for them . . .

I'm disappointed. They don't seem to have noticed me. They're all heading into town, as if a visiting spacecraft was an everyday occurrence . . . only a few left . . . maybe this will work . . . I suppose they can detect sound vibrations—most marine creatures can—though this atmosphere may be too thin to carry my voice very far . . .

FALCON—EXTERNAL SPEAKER . . .

HELLO, CAN YOU HEAR ME? MY NAME IS FRANK POOLE . . . AHEM . . . I COME IN PEACE FOR ALL MANKIND . . .

Makes me feel rather stupid, but can you suggest anything better? And it will be good for the record . . .

Nobody's taking the slightest notice. Big ones and little ones, they're all creeping toward their igloos. Wonder what they actually do when they get there—perhaps I should follow. I'm sure it would be perfectly safe—I can move so much faster—

I've just had an amusing flashback. All these creatures going in the same direction—they look like the commuters who used to surge back and forth twice a day between home and office, before electronics made it unnecessary.

Let's try again, before they all disappear . . .

HELLO THERE—THIS IS FRANK POOLE, A VISITOR FROM PLANET EARTH. CAN YOU HEAR ME?

I HEAR YOU, FRANK. THIS IS DAVE.

29. THE GHOSTS IN THE MACHINE

Frank Poole's immediate reaction was one of utter astonishment, followed by overwhelming joy. He had never really believed that he would make any kind of contact, either with the Europs or the Monolith. Indeed, he had even had fantasies of kicking in frustration against that towering ebon wall and shouting angrily, "Is there anybody at home?"

Yet he should not have been so amazed: some intelligence must have monitored his approach from Ganymede, and permitted him to land. He should have taken Ted Khan more seriously.

"Dave," he said slowly, "is that really you?"

Who else could it be? a part of his mind asked. Yet it was not a foolish question. There was something curiously mechanical—impersonal—about the voice that came from the small speaker on *Falcon*'s control board.

"Yes, Frank. I am Dave."

There was a very brief pause: then the same voice continued, without any change of intonation:

"Hello, Frank. This is Hal."

MISS PRINGLE
RECORD

Well—Indra, Dim—I'm glad I recorded all that, otherwise you'd never believe me . . .

I guess I'm still in a state of shock. First of all, how should I feel about someone who tried to—who did—kill me—even if it was a thousand years ago! But I understand now that Hal wasn't to blame; nobody was. There's a very good piece of advice I've often found useful: "Never attribute to malevolence what is merely due to incompetence." I can't feel any anger toward a bunch of programmers I never knew, who've been dead for centuries.

I'm glad this is encrypted, as I don't know how it should be handled, and a lot that I tell you may turn out to be complete nonsense. I'm already suffering from information overload, and had to ask Dave to leave me for a while—after all the trouble I've gone through to meet him! But I don't think I hurt his feelings: I'm not sure yet if he has any feelings . . .

What is he—good question! Well, he really is Dave Bowman, but with most of the humanity stripped away—like—ah—like the synopsis of a book or a technical paper. You know how an abstract can give all the basic information—but no hint of the author's personality? Yet there were moments when I felt that something of the old Dave was still there. I wouldn't go so far as to say he's pleased to meet me again—moderately satisfied might be more like it . . . For myself, I'm still very confused. Like meeting an old friend after a long separation, and finding that they're now a different person. Well, it has been a thousand years—and I can't imagine what experiences he's known, though as I'll show you presently, he's tried to share some of them with me.

And Hal—he's here too, without question. Most of the time, there's no way I can tell which of them is speaking to me. Aren't there examples of multiple personalities in the medical records? Maybe it's something like that.

I asked him how this had happened to them both, and he—they—dammit, Halman!—tried to explain. Let me repeat—I may have got it partly wrong, but it's the only working hypothesis I have.

Of course, the Monolith—in its various manifestations—is the key—no, that's the wrong word—didn't someone once say it was a kind of cosmic Swiss Army knife? You still have them, I've noticed, though both Switzerland and its army disappeared centuries ago. It's a general purpose device that can do anything it wants to. Or was programmed to do . . .

Back in Africa, four million years ago, it gave us that evolutionary kick in the pants, for better or for worse. Then its sibling on the Moon waited for us to climb out of the cradle. That we've already guessed, and Dave's confirmed it.

I said that he doesn't have many human feelings, but he still has curiosity—he wants to learn. And what an opportunity he's had!

When the Jupiter Monolith absorbed him—can't think of a better word—it got more than it bargained for. Though it used him—apparently as a captured specimen, and a probe to investigate Earth—he's also been using it. With Hal's assistance—and who should understand a supercomputer better than another one?—he's been exploring its memory, and trying to find its purpose.

Now, this is something that's very hard to believe. The Monolith is a fantastically powerful machine—look what it did to Jupiter!—but it's no more than that. It's running on automatic; it has no consciousness. I remember once thinking that I might have to kick the Great Wall and shout, "Is there anyone there?" And the correct answer would have to be—no one, except Dave and Hal . . .

Worse still, some of its systems may have started to fail; Dave even suggests that, in a fundamental way, it's become stupid! Perhaps it's been left on its own for too long—it's time for a service check.

And he believes the Monolith has made at least one misjudgment. Perhaps that's not the right word—it may have been deliberate, carefully considered . . .

In any event, it's—well, truly awesome, and terrifying in its implications. Luckily, I can show it to you, so you can decide for yourselves. Yes, even though it happened a thousand years ago, when *Leonov* flew the second mission to Jupiter! And all this time, no one has ever guessed . . .

I'm certainly glad you got me fitted with the Braincap. Of course it's been invaluable—I can't imagine life without it—but now it's doing a job it was never designed for. And doing it remarkably well.

It took Halman about ten minutes to find how it worked, and to set up an interface. Now we have mind-to-mind contact—which is quite a strain on me, I can tell you. I have to keep asking them to slow down, and use baby-talk. Or should I say baby-think . . .

I'm not sure how well this will come through. It's a thousand-year-old recording of Dave's own experience, somehow stored in the Monolith's enormous memory, then retrieved by Dave and injected into my Braincap—don't ask me exactly how—and finally transferred and beamed to you by Ganymede Central. Phew. Hope you don't get a headache downloading it.

Over to Dave Bowman at Jupiter, early Twenty-first Century . . .

30. FOAMSCAPE

The million-kilometer-long tendrils of magnetic force, the sudden explosions of radio waves, the geysers of electrified plasma wider than the planet Earth—they were as real and clearly visible to him as the clouds banding the planet in multihued glory. He could understand the complex pattern of their interactions, and realized that Jupiter was much more wonderful than anyone had ever guessed.

Even as he fell through the roaring heart of the Great Red Spot, with the lightning of its continent-wide thunderstorms detonating around him, he *knew* why it had persisted for centuries though it was made of gases far less substantial than those that formed the hurricanes of Earth. The thin scream of hydrogen wind faded as he sank into the calmer depths, and a sleet of waxen snowflakes—some already coalescing into barely palpable mountains of hydrocarbon foam—descended from the heights above. It was already warm enough for liquid water to exist, but there were no oceans there; this purely gaseous environment was too tenuous to support them.

He descended through layer after layer of cloud, until he entered a region of such clarity that even human vision could have scanned an area more than a thousand kilometers across. It was only a minor eddy in the vaster gyre of the Great Red Spot; and it held a secret that men had long guessed, but never proved.

Skirting the foothills of the drifting foam mountains were myriads of small, sharply defined clouds, all about the same size and patterned with similar red and brown mottlings. They were small only as compared with the inhuman scale of their surroundings; the very least would have covered a fair-size city.

They were clearly alive, for they were moving with slow deliberation along the flanks of the aerial mountains, browsing off their slopes like colossal sheep. And they were calling to each other in the meter band, their radio voices faint but clear against the cracklings and concussions of Jupiter itself.

Nothing less than living gasbags, they floated in the narrow zone between freezing heights and scorching depths. Narrow, yes—but a domain far larger than all the biosphere of Earth.

They were not alone. Moving swiftly among them were other creatures so small that they could easily have been overlooked. Some of them bore an almost uncanny resemblance to terrestrial aircraft and were of about the same size. But they too were alive—perhaps predators, perhaps parasites, perhaps even herdsmen.

A whole new chapter of evolution, as alien as that which he had glimpsed on Europa, was opening before him. There were jet-propelled torpedoes like the squids of the terrestrial oceans, hunting and devouring the huge gasbags. But the balloons were not defenseless; some of them fought back with electric thunderbolts and with clawed tentacles like kilometer-long chainsaws.

There were even stranger shapes, exploiting almost every possibility of geometry—bizarre, translucent kites, tetrahedra, spheres, polyhedra, tangles of twisted ribbons . . . The gigantic plankton of the Jovian atmosphere, they were designed to float like gossamer in the uprising currents, until they had lived long enough to reproduce; then they would be swept down into the depths to be carbonized and recycled in a new generation.

He was searching a world more than a hundred times the area of Earth, and though he saw many wonders, nothing there hinted of intelligence. The radio voices of the great balloons carried only simple messages of warning or of fear. Even the hunters, who might have been expected to develop higher degrees of organization, were like the sharks in Earth's oceans—mindless automata.

And for all its breathtaking size and novelty, the biosphere of Jupiter was a fragile world, a place of mists and foam, of delicate silken threads and paper-thin tissues spun from the continual snowfall of petrochemicals formed by lightning in the upper atmosphere. Few of its constructs were more substantial than soap bubbles; its most awesome predators could be torn to shreds by even the feeblest of terrestrial carnivores.

Like Europa on a vastly grander scale, Jupiter was an evolutionary cul-de-sac. Consciousness would never emerge here; even if it did, it would be doomed to a stunted existence. A purely aerial culture might develop, but in an environment where fire was impossible, and solids scarcely existed, it could never even reach the Stone Age.

31. NURSERY

MISS PRINGLE

RECORD

Well, Indra—Dim—I hope that came through in good shape—I still find it hard to believe. All those fantastic creatures—surely we should have detected their radio voices, even if we couldn't understand them!—wiped out in a moment, so that Jupiter could be made into a sun.

And now we can understand why. It was to give the Europs their chance. What pitiless logic: is intelligence the only thing that matters? I can see some long arguments with Ted Khan over this—

The next question is: will the Europs make the grade—or will they remain forever stuck in the kindergarten—not even that—the nursery? Though a thousand years is a very short time, one would have expected some progress, but according to Dave they're exactly the same now as when they left the sea. Perhaps that's the trouble; they still have one foot—or one twig!—in the water.

And here's another thing we got completely wrong. We thought they went back into the water to sleep. It's just the other way round—they go back to eat, and sleep when they come on land! As we might have guessed from their structure—that network of branches—they're plankton feeders . . .

I asked Dave, "What about the igloos they've built. Aren't they a technological advance?" And he said: not really—they're only adaptations of structures they make on the seabed, to protect themselves from various predators—especially something like a flying carpet, as big as a football field . . .

There's one area, though, where they have shown initiative—even creativity. They're fascinated by metals, presumably because they don't exist in pure form in the ocean. That's why *Tsien* was stripped—the same thing's happened to the occasional probes that have come down in their territory.

What do they do with the copper and beryllium and titanium they collect? Nothing useful, I'm afraid. They pile it all together in one place, in a fantastic heap that they keep reassembling. They could be developing an aesthetic sense—I've seen worse in the Museum of Modern Art . . . But I've got another theory—did you ever hear of cargo cults? During the Twentieth Century, some of the few primitive tribes that still existed made imitation airplanes out of bamboo, in the hope of attracting the big birds in the sky that occasionally brought them wonderful gifts. Perhaps the Europs have the same idea.

Now that question you keep asking me . . . What is Dave? And how did he—and Hal—become whatever it is they are now?

The quick answer, of course, is that they're both emulations—simulations—in the Monolith's gigantic memory. Most of the time they're inactivated; when I asked Dave about this, he said he'd been "awake"—his actual word—for only fifty years altogether, in the thousand since his, er, metamorphosis.

When I asked if he resented this takeover of his life, he said, "Why should I resent it? I am performing my functions perfectly." Yes, that sounds exactly like Hal! But I believe it was Dave—if there's any distinction now.

Remember that Swiss Army knife analogy? Halman is one of this cosmic knife's myriads of components.

But he's not a completely passive tool—when he's awake, he has some autonomy, some independence—presumably within limits set by the Monolith's overriding control. During the centuries, he's been used as a kind of intelligent probe to examine Jupiter—as you've just seen—as well as Ganymede and the Earth. That confirms those mysterious events in Florida, reported by Dave's old girlfriend, and the nurse who was looking after his mother, just moments before her death . . . as well as the encounters in Anubis City.

And it also explains another mystery. I asked Dave directly: "Why was I allowed to land on Europa, when everyone else has been turned away for centuries? I fully expected to be!"

The answer's ridiculously simple. The Monolith uses Dave—Halman—from time to time, to keep an eye on us. Dave knew all about my rescue—even saw some of the media interviews I made, on Earth and on Ganymede. I must say I'm still a little hurt he made no attempt to contact me! But at least he put out the Welcome mat when I did arrive . . .

Dim—I still have forty-eight hours before *Falcon* leaves—with or without me! I don't think I'll need them, now I've made contact with Halman; we can keep in touch just as easily from Anubis . . . if he wants to do so.

And I'm anxious to get back to the Grannymede as quickly as possible. *Falcon*'s a fine little spacecraft, but her plumbing could be improved—it's beginning to smell in here, and I'm itching for a shower.

Look forward to seeing you—and especially Ted Khan. We have much to talk about, before I return to Earth.

STORE
TRANSMIT

V. TERMINATION

The toil of all that be
Helps not the primal fault;
It rains into the sea,
And still the sea is salt.

A. E. HOUSMAN

MORE POEMS

32. A GENTLEMAN
OF LEISURE

On the whole, it had been an interesting but uneventful three decades, punctuated by the joys and sorrows that Time and Fate bring to all mankind. The greatest of those joys had been wholly unexpected; in fact, before he left Earth for Ganymede, Poole would have dismissed the very idea as preposterous.

There is much truth in the saying that absence makes the heart grow fonder. When he and Indra Wallace met again, they discovered that, despite their bantering and occasional disagreements, they were closer than they had imagined. One thing led to another—including, to their mutual joy, Dawn Wallace and Martin Poole.

It was rather late in life to start a family—quite apart from that little matter of a thousand years—and Professor Anderson had warned them that it might be impossible. Or even worse . . .

"You were lucky in more ways than you realize," he told Poole. "Radiation damage was surprisingly low, and we were able to make all essential repairs from your intact DNA. But until we do some more tests, I can't promise genetic integrity. So enjoy yourselves—but don't start a family until I give the O.K."

The tests had been time-consuming, and as Anderson had feared, further repairs were necessary. There was one major setback—something that could never have lived, even if it had been allowed to go beyond the first few weeks after conception—but Martin and Dawn were perfect, with just the right number of heads, arms, and legs. They were also handsome and intelligent, and barely managed to escape being spoiled by their doting parents—who continued to be the best of friends when, after fifteen years, each opted for independence again. Because of their Social Achievement Rating, they would have been permitted—indeed, encouraged—to have another child, but they decided not to put any more of a burden on their astonishingly good luck.

One tragedy had shadowed Poole's personal life during this period—and indeed, had shocked the whole Solar community. Captain Chandler and his entire crew had been lost when the nucleus of a comet they were reconnoitering exploded suddenly, destroying *Goliath* so completely that only a few fragments were ever located. Such explosions—caused by reactions among unstable molecules that existed at very low temperatures—were a well-known danger to comet-collectors, and Chandler had encountered several during his career. No one would ever know the exact circumstances that caused so experienced a spaceman to be taken by surprise.

Poole missed Chandler very badly: he had played a unique role in his life, and there was no one to replace him—no one, except Dave Bowman, with whom he had shared so momentous an adventure. They had often planned to go into space together again, perhaps all the way out to the Oort Cloud, with its unknown mysteries and its remote but inexhaustible wealth of ice. Yet some conflict of schedules had always upset their plans, so this was a wished-for future that would never exist.

Another long-desired goal Poole had managed to achieve—despite doctor's orders. He had been down to Earth: and once was quite enough.

The vehicle in which he had traveled looked almost identical to the wheelchairs used by the luckier paraplegics of his own time. It was motorized, and had balloon tires that allowed it to roll over reasonably smooth surfaces. However, it could also fly—at an altitude of about twenty centimeters—on an air-cushion produced by a set of small but very powerful fans. Poole was surprised that so primitive a technology was still in use, but inertia-control devices were too bulky for such small-scale applications.

Seated comfortably in his hoverchair, he was scarcely conscious of his increasing weight as he descended into the heart of Africa; though he did notice some difficulty in breathing, he had experienced far worse during his astronaut training. What he was not prepared for was the blast of furnace-heat that smote him as he rolled out of the gigantic, sky-piercing cylinder that formed the base of the Tower. Yet it was still morning: what would it be like at noon?

He had barely accustomed himself to the heat when his sense of smell was assailed. A myriad of odors—none unpleasant, but all unfamiliar—clamored for his attention. He closed his eyes for a few minutes, in an attempt to avoid overloading his input circuits.

Before he had decided to open them again, he felt some large, moist object palpating the back of his neck.

"Say hello to Elizabeth," said his guide, a burly young man dressed in traditional Great White Hunter garb, much too smart to have seen any real use: "She's our official greeter."

Poole twisted round in his chair, and found himself looking into the soulful eyes of a baby elephant.

"Hello, Elizabeth," he answered, rather feebly. Elizabeth lifted her trunk in salute, and emitted a sound not usually heard in polite society, though Poole felt sure it was well intentioned.

Altogether, he spent less than an hour on Planet Earth, skirting the edge of a jungle whose stunted trees compared unfavorably with Skyland's, and encountering much of the local fauna. His guide apologized for the friendliness of the lions, who had been spoiled by tourists—but the malevolent expressions of the crocodiles more than compensated; here was Nature raw and unchanged.

Before he returned to the Tower, Poole risked taking a few steps away from his hoverchair. He realized that this would be the equivalent of carrying his own weight on his back, but that did not seem an impossible feat, and he would never forgive himself unless he attempted it.

It was not a good idea; perhaps he should have tried it in a cooler climate. After no more than a dozen steps, he was glad to sink back into the luxurious clutches of the chair.

"That's enough," he said wearily. "Let's go back to the Tower."

As he rolled into the elevator lobby, he noticed a sign that he had somehow overlooked during the excitement of his arrival. It read:

WELCOME TO AFRICA!
"In wildness is the preservation of the world."
HENRY DAVID THOREAU (1817–1862)

Observing Poole's interest, the guide asked, "Did you know him?"

It was the sort of question Poole heard all too often, and at the moment he did not feel equipped to deal with it.

"I don't think so," he answered wearily, as the great doors closed behind them, shutting out the sights, scents, and sounds of Mankind's earliest home.

His vertical safari had satisfied his need to visit Earth, and he did his best to ignore the various aches and pains acquired there when he returned to his apartment at Level 10,000—a prestigious location, even in this democratic society. Indra, however, was mildly shocked by his appearance, and ordered him straight to bed.

"Just like Antaeus—but in reverse!" she muttered darkly.

"Who?" asked Poole: there were times when his wife's erudition was a little overwhelming, but he had determined never to let it give him an inferiority complex.

"Son of the Earth Goddess, Gaea. Hercules wrestled with him—but every time he was thrown to the ground, Antaeus renewed his strength."

"Who won?"

"Hercules, of course—by holding Antaeus in the air, so Ma couldn't recharge his batteries."

"Well, I'm sure it won't take me long to recharge mine. And I've learned one lesson. If I don't get more exercise, I may have to move up to Lunar Gravity level."

Poole's good resolution lasted a full month: every morning he went for a brisk five-kilometer walk, choosing a different level of the Africa Tower each day. Some floors were still vast, echoing deserts of metal that would probably never be occupied, but others had been land-scaped and developed over the centuries in a bewildering variety of architectural styles. Many were borrowings from past ages and cultures; others hinted at futures that Poole would not care to visit. At least there was no danger of boredom, and on many of his walks he was accompanied, at a respectful distance, by small groups of friendly children. They were seldom able to keep up with him for long.

One day, as Poole was striding down a convincing—though sparsely populated—imitation of the Champs Elysées, he suddenly spotted a familiar face.

"Danil!" he called.

The other man took not the slightest notice, even when Poole called again, more loudly.

"Don't you remember me?"

Danil—and now that he had caught up with him, Poole did not have the slightest doubt of his identity—looked genuinely baffled.

"I'm sorry," he said. "You're Commander Poole, of course. But I'm sure we've never met before."

Now it was Poole's turn to be embarrassed.

"Stupid of me," he apologized. "Must have mistaken you for someone else. Have a good day."

He was glad of the encounter, and was pleased to know that Danil was back in normal society. Whether his original crime had been ax murders or overdue library books should no longer be the concern of his onetime employer; the account had been settled, the books closed. Although Poole sometimes missed the cops-and-robbers dramas he had often enjoyed in his youth, he had grown to accept the current wisdom: excessive interest in pathological behavior was itself pathological.

With the help of Miss Pringle, Mk III, Poole had been able to schedule his life so that there were even occasional blank moments when he could relax and set his Braincap on Random Search, scanning his areas of interest. Outside his immediate family, his chief concern was still among the moons of Jupiter/Lucifer, not least because he was recognized as the leading expert on the subject, and a permanent member of the Europa Committee.

This had been set up almost a thousand years ago, to consider what, if anything, could and should be done about the mysterious satellite. Over the centuries, it had accumulated a vast amount of information, going all the way back to the *Voyager* flybys of 1979 and the first detailed surveys from the orbiting *Galileo* spacecraft of 1996—the very year Poole had been born.

Like most long-lived organizations, the Europa Committee had become slowly fossilized, and now met only when there was some new development. It had woken up with a start after Halman's reappearance, and appointed an energetic new chairperson whose first act had been to co-opt Poole.

Though there was little that he could contribute that was not already recorded, Poole was very happy to be on the Committee. It was obviously his duty to make himself available, and it also gave him an official position he would otherwise have lacked. Previously his status was what had once been called a "national treasure," which he found faintly embarrassing. Although he was glad to be supported in luxury by a world wealthier than all the dreams war-ravaged earlier ages could have imagined, he felt the need to justify his existence.

He also felt another need, which he seldom articulated even to himself. Halman had spoken to him, if only briefly, at their strange encounter two decades ago. Poole was certain that he could easily do so again, if he wished. Were all human contacts no longer of interest to him? He hoped that was not the case; yet that might be one explanation for his silence.

He was frequently in touch with Theodore Khan—as active and acerbic as ever, and now the Europa Committee's representative on Ganymede. Ever since Poole had returned to Earth, Khan had been trying in vain to open a channel of communication with Bowman. He could not understand why long lists of important questions on subjects of vital philosophical and historic interest received not even brief acknowledgments.

"Does the Monolith keep your friend Halman so busy that he can't talk to me?" he complained to Poole. "What does he do with his time, anyway?"

It was a very reasonable question; and the answer came, like a thunderbolt out of a cloudless sky, from Bowman himself—as a perfectly commonplace vidphone call.

33. CONTACT

"Hello, Frank. This is Dave. I have a very important message for you. I assume that you are now in your suite in Africa Tower. If you are there, please identify yourself by giving the name of our instructor in orbital mechanics. I will wait for sixty seconds, and if there is no reply will try again in exactly one hour."

That minute was hardly long enough for Poole to recover from the shock. He felt a brief surge of delight, as well as astonishment, before another emotion took over. Glad though he was to hear from Bowman again, that phrase "a very important message" sounded distinctly ominous.

At least it was fortunate, Poole told himself, that he'd asked for one of the few names I can remember. Yet who could forget a Scot with a Glasgow accent so thick it had taken them a week to master it? But he had been a brilliant lecturer—once you understood what he was saying.

"Dr. Gregory McVitty."

"Accepted. Now please switch on your Braincap receiver. It will take three minutes to download this message. Do not attempt to monitor: I am using ten to one compression. I will wait two minutes before starting."

How is he managing to do this? Poole wondered. Jupiter/Lucifer was now over fifty light-minutes away, so this message must have left almost an hour ago. It must have been sent with an intelligent agent in a properly addressed package on the Ganymede–Earth beam—but that would have been a trivial feat to Halman, with the resources he had apparently been able to tap inside the Monolith.

The indicator light on the Brainbox was flickering. The message was coming through.

At the compression Halman was using, it would take half an hour for Poole to absorb the message in real time. But he needed only ten minutes to know that his peaceful lifestyle had come to an abrupt end.

34. JUDGMENT

In a world of universal and instantaneous communication, it was very difficult to keep secrets. This was a matter, Poole decided immediately, for face-to-face discussion.

The Europa Committee had grumbled, but all its members had assembled in his apartment. There were seven of them—the lucky number, doubtless suggested by the phases of the Moon, that had always fascinated mankind. It was the first time Poole had met three of the Committee's members, though by now he knew them all more thoroughly than he could possibly have done in a pre-Braincapped lifetime.

"Chairperson Oconnor, members of the Committee—I'd like to say a few words—only a few, I promise!—before you download this message I've received from Europa. And this is something I prefer to do verbally; that's more natural for me—I'm afraid I'll never be quite at ease with direct mental transfer.

"As you all know, Dave Bowman and Hal have been stored as emulations in the Monolith on Europa. Apparently it never discards a tool it had once found useful, and from time to time it activates Halman, to monitor our affairs—when they begin to concern it. As I suspect, my arrival may have done—though perhaps I flatter myself!

"But Halman isn't just a passive tool. The Dave component still retains something of its human origins—even emotions. And because we were trained together—shared almost everything for years—he apparently finds it much easier to communicate with me than with anyone else. I would like to think he enjoys doing it, but perhaps that's too strong a word . . .

"He's also curious—inquisitive—and perhaps a little resentful of the way he's been collected, like a specimen of wildlife. Though that's probably what we are, from the viewpoint of the intelligence that created the Monolith.

"And where is that intelligence now? Halman apparently knows the answer, and it's a chilling one.

"As we always suspected, the Monolith is part of a galactic network of some kind. And the nearest node—the Monolith's controller, or immediate superior—is 450 light-years away.

"Much too close for comfort! This means that the report on us and our affairs that was transmitted early in the Twenty-first Century was received half a millennium ago. If the Monolith's—let's say Supervisor—replied at once, any further instructions should be arriving just about now.

"And that's exactly what seems to be happening. During the last few days, the Monolith has been receiving a continuous string of messages, and has been setting up new programs, presumably in accordance with these.

"Unfortunately, Halman can only make guesses about the nature of those instructions. As you'll gather when you've downloaded this tablet, he has some limited access to many of the Monolith's circuits and memory banks, and can even carry on a kind of dialogue with it. If that's the right word—since you need two people for that! I still can't really grasp the idea that the Monolith, for all its powers, doesn't possess consciousness—doesn't even know that it exists!

"Halman's been brooding over the problem for a thousand years—on and off—and has come to the same answer that most of us have done. But his conclusion must surely carry far more weight, because of his inside knowledge.

"Sorry! I wasn't intending to make a joke—but what else could you call it?

"Whatever went to the trouble of creating us—or at least tinkering with our ancestors' minds and genes—is deciding what to do next. And Halman is pessimistic. No—that's an exaggeration. Let's say he doesn't think much of our chances, but is now too detached an observer to be unduly worried. The future—the survival!—of the human race isn't much more than an interesting problem to him, but he's willing to help."

Poole suddenly stopped talking, to the surprise of his intent audience.

"That's strange. I've just had an amazing flashback . . . I'm sure it explains what's happening. Please bear with me . . .

"Dave and I were walking together one day, along the beach at the Cape, a few weeks before launch, when we noticed a large beetle lying on the sand. As often happens, it had fallen on its back and was waving its legs in the air, struggling to get right-way-up.

"I ignored it—we were engaged in some complicated technical discussion—but not Dave. He stepped aside, and carefully flipped it over with his shoe. As it flew away I commented, 'Are you sure that was a good idea? Now it will go off and chomp somebody's prize chrysanthemums.' And he answered, 'Maybe you're right. But I'd like to give it the benefit of the doubt.'

"My apologies—I'd promised to say only a few words! But I'm very glad I remembered that incident: I really believe it puts Halman's message in the right perspective. He's giving the human race the benefit of the doubt . . .

"Now please check your Braincaps. This is a high-density recording—top of the U.V. band, Channel 110. Make yourselves comfortable, but be sure you're in line of sight. Here we go . . ."

35. COUNCIL OF WAR

No one asked for a replay. Once was sufficient.

There was a brief silence when the playback finished; then Chairperson Dr. Oconnor removed her Braincap, massaged her shining scalp, and said slowly:

"You taught me a phrase from your period that seems very appropriate now. This is a can of worms."

"But only Bowman—Halman—has opened it," said one of the Committee members. "Does he really understand the operation of something as complex as the Monolith? Or is this whole scenario a figment of his imagination?"

"I don't think he has much imagination," Dr. Oconnor answered. "And everything checks perfectly. Especially the reference to Nova Scorpio. We assumed that was an accident; apparently it was a—judgment."

"First Jupiter—now Scorpio," said Dr. Kraussman, the distinguished physicist who was popularly regarded as a reincarnation of the legendary Einstein. A little plastic surgery, it was rumored, had also helped. "Who will be next in line?"

"We always guessed," said the Chair, "that the TMAs were monitoring us." She paused for a moment, then added ruefully: "What bad—what incredibly bad!—luck that the final report went off, just after the very worst period in human history!"

There was another silence. Everyone knew that the Twentieth Century had often been branded "The Century of Torture."

Poole listened without interrupting, while he waited for some consensus to emerge. Not for the first time, he was impressed by the quality of the Committee. No one was trying to prove a pet theory, score debating points, or inflate an ego: he could not help drawing a contrast with the often bad-tempered arguments he had heard in his own time, between Space Agency engineers and administrators, congressional staffs, and industrial executives.

Yes, the human race had undoubtedly improved. The Braincap had not only helped to weed out misfits, but had enormously increased the efficiency of education. Yet there had also been a loss; there were very few memorable characters in this society. Offhand he could think of only four—Indra, Captain Chandler, Dr. Khan, and the Dragon Lady of wistful memory.

The Chairperson let the discussion flow smoothly back and forth until everyone had had a say, then began her summing up.

"The obvious first question—how seriously should we take this threat—isn't worth wasting time on. Even if it's a false alarm, or a misunderstanding, it's potentially so grave that we must assume it's real, until we have absolute proof to the contrary. Agreed?

"Good. And we don't know how much time we have. So we must assume that the danger is immediate. Perhaps Halman may be able to give us some further warning, but by then it may be too late.

"So the only thing we have to decide is: how can we protect ourselves, against something as powerful as the Monolith? Look what happened to Jupiter! And, apparently, Nova Scorpio . . .

"I'm sure that brute force would be useless, though perhaps we should explore that option. Dr. Kraussman—how long would it take to build a super-bomb?"

"Assuming that the designs still exist, so that no research is necessary—oh, perhaps two weeks. Thermonuclear weapons are rather simple, and use common materials—after all, they made them back in the Second Millennium! But if you wanted something sophisticated—say an antimatter bomb, or a mini-black-hole—well, that might take a few months."

"Thank you; could you start looking into it? But as I've said, I don't believe it would work; surely something that can handle such powers must also be able to protect itself against them. So—any other suggestions?"

"Can we negotiate?" one councillor asked, not very hopefully.

"With what . . . or whom?" Kraussman answered. "As we've discovered, the Monolith is essentially a pure mechanism, doing just what it's been programmed to do. Perhaps that program has some degree of flexibility, but there's no way we can tell. And we certainly can't appeal to the Head Office—that's half a thousand light-years away!"

Poole listened without interrupting; there was nothing he could contribute to the discussion, and indeed much of it was completely over his head. He began to feel an insidious sense of depression; would it have been better, he wondered, not to pass on this information? Then, if it was a false alarm, no one would be any the worse. And if it was not—well, humanity would still have peace of mind, before whatever inescapable doom awaited it.

He was still mulling over these gloomy thoughts when he was suddenly alerted by a familiar phrase.

A quiet little member of the Committee, with a name so long and difficult that Poole had never been able to remember, much less pronounce it, had abruptly dropped just two words into the discussion.

"Trojan horse!"

There was one of those silences generally described as "pregnant," then a chorus of "Why didn't I think of that!" "Of course!" "Very good idea!" until the Chairperson, for the first time in the session, had to call for order.

"Thank you, Professor Thirugnanasampanthamoorthy," said Dr. Oconnor, without missing a beat. "Would you like to be more specific?"

"Certainly. If the Monolith is indeed, as everyone seems to think, essentially a machine without consciousness—and hence with only limited self-monitoring ability—we may already have the weapons that can defeat it. Locked up in the Vault."

"And a delivery system—Halman!"

"Precisely."

"Just a minute, Dr. T. We know nothing—absolutely nothing—about the Monolith's architecture. How can we be sure that anything our primitive species ever designed would be effective against it?"

"We can't—but remember this. However sophisticated it is, the Monolith has to obey exactly the same universal laws of logic that Aristotle and Boole formulated, centuries ago. That's why it may—no, should!—be vulnerable to the things locked up in the Vault. We have to assemble them in such a way that at least one of them will work. It's our only hope—unless anybody can suggest a better alternative."

"Excuse me," said Poole, finally losing patience. "Will someone kindly tell me—what and where is this famous Vault you're talking about?"

36. CHAMBER OF HORRORS

History is full of nightmares, some natural, some man-made.

By the end of the Twenty-first Century, most of the natural ones—smallpox, the Black Death, AIDS, the hideous viruses lurking in the African jungle—had been eliminated, or at least brought under control, by the advance of medicine. However, it was never wise to underestimate the ingenuity of Mother Nature, and no one doubted that the future would still have unpleasant biological surprises in store for mankind.

It seemed a sensible precaution, therefore, to keep a few specimens of all these horrors for scientific study—carefully guarded, of course, so that there was no possibility of them escaping and again wreaking havoc on the human race. But how could one be absolutely sure that there was no danger of this happening?

There had been—understandably—quite an outcry in the late Twentieth Century when it was proposed to keep the last known smallpox viruses at Disease Control Centers in the United States and Russia. However unlikely it might be, there was a finite possibility that they might be released by such accidents as earthquakes, equipment failures—or even deliberate sabotage by terrorist groups.

A solution that satisfied everyone (except a few "Preserve the lunar wilderness!" extremists) was to ship them to the Moon, and to keep them in a laboratory at the end of a kilometer-long shaft drilled into the isolated mountain Pico, one of the most prominent features of the Mare Imbrium. And here, over the years, they were joined by some of the most outstanding examples of misplaced human ingenuity—indeed, insanity.

There were gases and mists that, even in microscopic doses, caused slow or instant death. Some had been created by religious cultists who, though mentally deranged, had managed to acquire considerable scientific knowledge. Many of them believed that the end of the world was at hand (when, of course, only their followers would be saved). In case God was absentminded enough not to perform as scheduled, they wanted to make sure that they could rectify His unfortunate oversight.

The first assaults of these lethal cultists were made on such vulnerable targets as crowded subways, World Fairs, sports stadiums, pop concerts . . . tens of thousands were killed, and many more injured, before the madness was brought under control in the early Twenty-first Century. As often happens, some good came out of evil, because it forced the world's law-enforcement agencies to cooperate as never before. Even rogue states that had promoted political terrorism were unable to tolerate this random and wholly unpredictable variety.

The chemical and biological agents used in these attacks—as well as in earlier forms of warfare—joined the deadly collection in Pico. Their antidotes, when they existed, were also stored with them. It was hoped that none of this material would ever concern humanity again—but it was still available, under heavy guard, if it was needed in some desperate emergency.

The third category of items stored in the Pico Vault, although they could be classified as plagues, had never killed or injured anyone—directly. They had not even existed before the late Twentieth Century, but in a few decades they had done billions of dollars' worth of damage, and often wrecked lives as effectively as any bodily illness could have done. They were the diseases that attacked mankind's newest and most versatile servant, the computer.

Taking names from the medical dictionaries—viruses, prions, tapeworms—they were programs that often mimicked, with uncanny accuracy, the behavior of their organic relatives. Some were harmless—little more than playful jokes, contrived to surprise or amuse computer operators by unexpected messages and images on their visual displays. Others were far more malicious—deliberately designed agents of catastrophe.

In most cases their purpose was entirely mercenary; they were the weapons that sophisticated criminals used to blackmail the banks and commercial organizations that now depended utterly upon the efficient operation of their computer systems. On being warned that their data banks would be erased automatically at a certain time, unless they transferred a few megadollars to some anonymous offshore number, most victims decided not to risk possibly irreparable disaster. They paid up quietly, often—to avoid public or even private embarrassment—without notifying the police.

This understandable desire for privacy made it easy for the network highwaymen to conduct their electronic holdups: even when they were caught, they were treated gently by legal systems that did not know how to handle such novel crimes—and, after all, they had not really hurt anyone, had they? Indeed, after they had served their brief sentences, many of the perpetrators were quietly hired by their victims, on the old principle that poachers make the best gamekeepers.

These computer criminals were driven purely by greed, and certainly did not wish to destroy the organizations they preyed upon: no sensible parasite kills its host. But there were other, and much more dangerous, enemies of society at work . . .

Usually, they were maladjusted individuals—typically adolescent males—working entirely alone, and of course in complete secrecy. Their aim was to create programs that would simply create havoc and confusion, when they had been spread over the planet by the worldwide cable and radio networks, or on physical carriers such as diskettes and CD–ROMS. Then they would enjoy the resulting chaos, basking in the sense of power it gave their pitiful psyches.

Sometimes, these perverted geniuses were discovered and adopted by national intelligence agencies for their own secretive purposes—usually, to break into the data banks of their rivals. This was a fairly harmless line of employment, as the organizations concerned did at least have some sense of civic responsibility.

Not so the apocalyptic sects, who were delighted to discover this new armory, holding weapons far more effective, and more easily disseminated, than gas or germs. And much more difficult to counter, since they could be broadcast instantaneously to millions of offices and homes.

The collapse of the New York–Havana Bank in 2005, the launching of Indian nuclear missiles in 2007 (luckily with their warheads unactivated), the shutdown of Pan-European Air Traffic Control in 2008, the paralysis of the North American telephone network in that same year—all these were cult-inspired rehearsals for Doomsday. Thanks to brilliant feats of counterintelligence by normally uncooperative, and even warring, national agencies, this menace was slowly brought under control.

At least, so it was generally believed: there had been no serious attacks at the very foundations of society for several hundred years. One of the chief weapons of victory had been the Braincap—though there were some who believed that this achievement had been bought at too great a cost.

Though arguments over the freedom of the Individual versus the duties of the State were old when Plato and Aristotle attempted to codify them, and would probably continue until the end of time, some consensus had been reached in the Third Millennium. It was generally agreed that Communism was the most perfect form of government; unfortunately, it had been demonstrated—at the cost of some hundreds of millions of lives—that it was only applicable to social insects, Robots Class II, and similar restricted categories. For imperfect human beings, the least-worse answer was Democracy, frequently defined as "Individual greed, moderated by an efficient but not too zealous government."

Soon after the Braincap came into general use, some highly intelligent—and maximally zealous—bureaucrats realized that it had a unique potential as an early-warning system. During the setting-up process, when the new wearer was being mentally "calibrated," it was possible to detect many forms of psychosis before they had a chance of becoming dangerous. Often this suggested the best therapy, but when no cure appeared possible the subject could be electronically tagged—or, in extreme cases, segregated from society. Of course, this mental monitoring could test only those who were fitted with a Braincap—but by the end of the Third Millennium this was as essential for everyday life as the personal telephone had been at its beginning. In fact, anyone who did not join the vast majority was automatically suspect, and checked as a potential deviant.

Needless to say, when "Mind-probing," as its critics called it, started coming into general use, there were cries of outrage from civil rights organizations; one of their most effective slogans was "Braincap or Braincop?" Slowly—even reluctantly—it was accepted that this form of monitoring was a necessary precaution against far worse evils; and it was no coincidence that with the general improvement in mental health, religious fanaticism also started its rapid decline.

When the long-drawn-out war against the cybernet criminals ended, the victors found themselves owning an embarrassing collection of spoils, all of them utterly incomprehensible to any past conqueror. There were, of course, hundreds of computer viruses, most of them very difficult to detect and kill. And here were some entities—for want of a better name—that were much more terrifying. They were brilliantly invented diseases for which there was no cure—in some cases, not even the possibility of a cure . . .

Many of them had been linked to great mathematicians who would have been horrified by this corruption of their discoveries. As it is a human characteristic to belittle a real danger by giving it an absurd name, the designations were often facetious: the Godel Gremlin, the Mandelbrot Maze, the Combinatorial Catastrophe, the Transfinite Trap, the Conway Conundrum, the Turing Torpedo, the Lorenz Labyrinth, the Boolean Bomb, the Shannon Snare, the Cantor Cataclysm . . .

If any generalization was possible, all these mathematical horrors operated on the same principle. They did not depend for their effectiveness on anything as naive as memory-erasure or code corruption—on the contrary. Their approach was more subtle; they persuaded their host machine to initiate a program that could not be completed before the end of the universe, or that—the Mandelbrot Maze was the deadliest example—involved a literally infinite series of steps.

A trivial example would be the calculation of Pi, or any other irrational number. However, even the most stupid electro-optic computer would not fall into such a simple trap: the day had long since passed when mechanical morons would wear out their gears, grinding them to powder as they tried to divide by zero . . .

The challenge to the demon programmers was to convince their targets that the task set them had a definite conclusion that could be reached in a finite time. In the battle of wits between man (seldom woman, despite such role models as Lady Ada Lovelace, Admiral Grace Hopper, and Dr. Susan Calvin) and machine, the machine almost invariably lost.

It would have been possible—though in some cases difficult and even risky—to destroy the captured obscenities by ERASE/OVERWRITE commands, but they represented an enormous investment in time and ingenuity that, however misguided, seemed a pity to waste. And, more important, perhaps they should be kept for study, in some secure location, as a safeguard against the time when some evil genius might reinvent and deploy them.

The solution was obvious. The digital demons should be sealed with their chemical and biological counterparts, hopefully forever, in the Pico Vault.

37. OPERATION DAMOCLES

Poole never had much contact with the team that assembled the weapon everyone hoped would never have to be used. The operation—ominously, but aptly, named DAMOCLES—was so highly specialized that he could contribute nothing directly, and he saw enough of the task force to realize that some of them might almost belong to an alien species. Indeed, one key member was apparently in a lunatic asylum—Poole had been surprised to find that such places still existed—and Chairperson Oconnor sometimes suggested that at least two others should join him.

"Have you ever heard of the Enigma Project?" she remarked to Poole, after a particularly frustrating session.

When he shook his head, she continued: "I'm surprised—it was only a few decades before you were born: I came across it when I was researching material for DAMOCLES. Very similar problem—in one of your wars, a group of brilliant mathematicians was gathered together, in great secrecy, to break an enemy code . . . incidentally, they built one of the very first real computers, to make the job possible.

"And there's a lovely story—I hope it's true—that reminds me of our own little team. One day the Prime Minister came on a visit of inspection, and afterward he said to Enigma's Director: 'When I told you to leave no stone unturned to get the men you needed, I didn't expect you to take me so literally.' "

Presumably all the right stones had been turned for Project DAMOCLES. However, as no one knew whether they were working against a deadline of days, weeks, or years, at first it was hard to generate any sense of urgency. The need for secrecy also created problems; since there was no point in spreading alarm throughout the Solar System, not more than fifty people knew of the project. But they were the people who mattered—who could marshal all the forces necessary, and who alone could authorize the opening of the Pico Vault, for the first time in five hundred years.

When Halman reported that the Monolith was receiving messages with increasing frequency, there seemed little doubt that something was going to happen. Poole was not the only one who found it hard to sleep in those days, even with the help of the Braincap's anti-insomnia programs. Before he finally did get to sleep, he often wondered if he would wake up again. But at last all the components of the weapon were assembled—a weapon invisible, untouchable—and unimaginable to almost all the warriors who had ever lived.

Nothing could have looked more harmless and innocent than the perfectly standard terabyte memory tablet, used with millions of Braincaps every day. But the fact that it was encased in a massive block of crystalline material, crisscrossed with metal bands, indicated that it was something quite out of the ordinary.

Poole received it with reluctance; he wondered if the courier who had been given the awesome task of carrying the Hiroshima atom bomb's core to the Pacific airbase from which it was launched had felt the same way. And yet, if all their fears were justified, his responsibility might be even greater.

And he could not be certain that even the first part of his mission would be successful. Because no circuit could be absolutely secure, Halman had not yet been informed about Project DAMOCLES; Poole would do that when he returned to Ganymede.

Then he could only hope that Halman would be willing to play the role of Trojan horse—and, perhaps, be destroyed in the process.

38. PREEMPTIVE STRIKE

It was strange to be back in the Hotel Grannymede after all these years—strangest of all, because it seemed completely unchanged, despite everything that had happened. Poole was still greeted by the familiar image of Bowman as he walked into the suite named after him: and, as he expected, Bowman/Halman was waiting, looking slightly less substantial than the ancient hologram.

Before they could even exchange greetings, there was an interruption that Poole would have welcomed—at any other time than this. The room vidphone gave its urgent trio of rising notes—also unchanged since his last visit—and an old friend appeared on the screen.

"Frank!" cried Theodore Khan, "why didn't you tell me you were coming! When can we meet? Why no video—someone with you? And who were all those official-looking types who landed at the same time—"

"Please Ted! Yes, I'm sorry—but believe me, I've got very good reasons—I'll explain later. And I do have someone with me—call you back just as soon as I can. Goodbye!"

As he belatedly gave the "Do Not Disturb" order, Poole said apologetically: "Sorry about that—you know who it was, of course."

"Yes—Dr. Khan. He often tried to get in touch with me."

"But you never answered. May I ask why?" Though there were far more important matters to worry about, Poole could not resist putting the question.

"Ours was the only channel I wished to keep open. Also, I was often away. Sometimes for years."

That was surprising—yet it should have not been. Poole knew well enough that Halman had been reported in many places, in many times. Yet—"away for years"? He might have visited quite a few star systems—perhaps that was how he knew about Nova Scorpio, only forty light-years distant. But he could never have gone all the way to the Node; there and back would have been a nine-hundred-year journey.

"How lucky that you were here when we needed you!"

It was very unusual for Halman to hesitate before replying. There was much longer than the unavoidable three-second time lag before he said slowly: "Are you sure that it was luck?"

"What do you mean?"

"I do not wish to talk about it, but twice I have—glimpsed—powers . . . entities—far superior to the Monoliths, and perhaps even their makers. We may both have less freedom than we imagine."

That was indeed a chilling thought; Poole needed a deliberate effort of will to put it aside and concentrate on the immediate problem.

"Let us hope we have enough free will to do what is necessary. Perhaps this is a foolish question. Does the Monolith know that we are meeting? Could it be—suspicious?"

"It is not capable of such an emotion. It has numerous fault-protection devices, some of which I understand. But that is all."

"Could it be overhearing us now?"

"I do not believe so."

I wish that I could be sure it was such a naive and simpleminded super-genius, thought Poole as he unlocked his briefcase and took out the sealed box containing the tablet. In this low gravity its weight was almost negligible; it was impossible to believe that it might hold the destiny of mankind.

"There was no way we could be certain of getting a secure circuit to you, so we couldn't go into details. This tablet contains programs that we hope will prevent the Monolith from carrying out any orders that threaten mankind. There are twenty of the most devastating viruses ever designed, most of which have no known antidote; in some cases, it is believed that none is possible. There are five copies of each. We would like you to release them when—and if—you think it is necessary. Dave—Hal—no one has ever been given such a responsibility. But we have no other choice."

Once again, the reply seemed to take longer than the three-second round-trip from Europa.

"If we do this, all the Monolith's functions may cease. We are uncertain what will happen to us then."

"We have considered that, of course. But by this time, you must surely have many facilities at your command—some of them probably beyond our understanding. I am also sending you a petabyte memory tablet. Ten to the fifteenth bytes is more than sufficient to hold all the memories and experiences of many lifetimes. This will give you one escape route: I suspect you have others."

"Correct. We will decide which to use at the appropriate time."

Poole relaxed—as far as was possible in this extraordinary situation. Halman was willing to cooperate: he still had sufficient links with his origins.

"Now, we have to get this tablet to you—physically. Its contents are too dangerous to risk sending over any radio or optical channel. I know you possess long-range control of matter: did you not once detonate an orbiting bomb? Could you transport it to Europa? Alternatively, we could send it in an auto-courier, to any point you specify."

"That would be best: I will collect it in Tsienville. Here are the coordinates . . ."

Poole was still slumped in his chair when the Bowman Suite monitor admitted the head of the delegation that had accompanied him from Earth. Whether Colonel Jones was a genuine colonel—or even if his name was Jones—were minor mysteries that Poole was not really interested in solving; it was sufficient that he was a superb organizer and had handled the mechanics of Operation DAMOCLES with quiet efficiency.

"Well, Frank—it's on its way. Will be landing in one hour, ten minutes. I assume that Halman can take it from there, but I don't understand how he can actually handle—is that the right word?—these tablets."

"I wondered about that, until someone on the Europa Committee explained it. There's a well-known—though not to me!—theorem stating that any computer can emulate any other computer. So I'm sure that Halman knows exactly what he's doing. He would never have agreed otherwise."

"I hope you're right," replied the colonel. "If not—well, I don't know what alternative we have."

There was a gloomy pause, until Poole did his best to relieve the tension.

"By the way, have you heard the local rumor about our visit?"

"Which particular one?"

"That we're a special commission sent here to investigate crime and corruption in this raw frontier township. The Mayor and the Sheriff are supposed to be running scared."

"How I envy them," said Colonel Jones. "Sometimes it's quite a relief to have something trivial to worry about."

39. DEICIDE

Like all the inhabitants of Anubis City (pop. now 56,521), Dr. Theodore Khan woke soon after local midnight to the sound of the General Alarm. His first reaction was, "Not another Icequake, for Deus' sake!"

He rushed to the window, shouting "Open" so loudly that the room did not understand, and he had to repeat the order in a normal voice. The light of Lucifer should have come streaming in, painting the patterns on the floor that so fascinated visitors from Earth, because they never moved even a fraction of a millimeter, no matter how long they waited . . .

That unvarying beam of light was no longer there. As Khan stared in utter disbelief through the huge, transparent bubble of the Anubis Dome, he saw a sky that Ganymede had not known for a thousand years. It was once more ablaze with stars; Lucifer had gone.

And then, as he explored the forgotten constellations, Khan noticed something even more terrifying. Where Lucifer should have been was a tiny disk of absolute blackness, eclipsing the unfamiliar stars.

There was only one possible explanation, Khan told himself numbly. Lucifer has been swallowed by a Black Hole. And it may be our turn next.

On the balcony of the Grannymede Hotel, Poole was watching the same spectacle, but with more complex emotions. Even before the General Alarm, his comsec had woken him with a message from Halman.

"It is beginning. We have infected the Monolith. But one—perhaps several—of the viruses have entered our own circuits. We do not know if we will be able to use the memory tablet you have given us. If we succeed, we will meet you in Tsienville."

Then came the surprising and strangely moving words whose exact emotional content would be debated for generations:

"If we are unable to download, remember us."

From the room behind him, Poole heard the voice of the Mayor, doing his best to reassure the now sleepless citizens of Anubis. Though he opened with that most terrifying of official statements— "No cause for alarm"—the Mayor did indeed have words of comfort.

"We don't know what's happening—but Lucifer's still shining normally! I repeat—Lucifer is still shining! We've just received news from the interorbit shuttle *Alcyone,* which left for Callisto half an hour ago. Here's their view—"

Poole left the balcony and rushed into his room just in time to see Lucifer blaze reassuringly on the vidscreen.

"What's happened," the Mayor continued breathlessly, "is that something has caused a temporary eclipse—we'll zoom in to look at it . . . Callisto Observatory, come in please . . ."

How does he know it's "temporary"? thought Poole, as he waited for the next image to come up on the screen.

Lucifer vanished, to be replaced by a field of stars. At the same time, the Mayor faded out and another voice took over:

"—two-meter telescope, but almost any instrument will do. It's a disk of perfectly black material, just over ten thousand kilometers across, so thin it shows no visible thickness. And it's placed exactly— obviously deliberately—to block Ganymede from receiving any light.

"We'll zoom in to see if it shows any details, though I rather doubt it . . ."

From the viewpoint of Callisto, the occulting disk was foreshortened into an oval, twice as long as it was wide. It expanded until it completely filled the screen; thereafter, it was impossible to tell whether the image was being zoomed, as it showed no structure whatsoever.

"As I thought—there's nothing to see. Let's pan over to the edge of the thing . . ."

Again there was no sense of motion, until a field of stars suddenly appeared, sharply defined by the curving edge of the world-sized disk. It was exactly as if they were looking past the horizon of an airless, perfectly smooth planet.

No, it was not perfectly smooth . . .

"That's interesting," commented the astronomer, who until now had sounded remarkably matter-of-fact, as if this sort of thing was an everyday occurrence. "The edge looks jagged—but in a very regular fashion—like a saw-blade . . ."

A circular saw, Poole muttered under his breath. Is it going to carve us up? Don't be ridiculous . . .

"This is as close as we can get before diffraction spoils the image— we'll process it later and get much better detail."

The magnification was now so great that all trace of the disk's circularity had vanished. Across the vidscreen was a black band, serrated along its edge with triangles so identical that Poole found it hard to avoid the ominous analogy of a saw-blade. Yet something else was nagging at the back of his mind . . .

Like everyone else on Ganymede, he watched the infinitely more distant stars drifting in and out of those geometrically perfect valleys. Very probably, many others jumped to the same conclusion even before he did.

If you attempt to make a disk out of rectangular blocks—whether their proportions are 1:4:9 or any other—it cannot possibly have a smooth edge. Of course, you can make it as near a perfect circle as you like, by using smaller and smaller blocks. Yet why go to that trouble, if you merely wanted to build a screen large enough to eclipse a sun?

The Mayor was right; the eclipse was indeed temporary. But its ending was the precise opposite of a solar one.

First light broke through at the exact center, not in the usual necklace of Bailey's Beads along the very edge. Jagged lines radiated from a dazzling pinhole—and now, under the highest magnification, the structure of the disk was being revealed. It was composed of millions of identical rectangles, perhaps the same size as the Great Wall of Europa. And now they were splitting apart: it was as if a gigantic jigsaw puzzle was being dismantled.

Its perpetual, but now briefly interrupted, daylight was slowly returning to Ganymede, as the disk fragmented and the rays of Lucifer poured through the widening gaps. Now the components themselves were evaporating, almost as if they needed the reinforcement of each other's contact to maintain reality.

Although it seemed like hours to the anxious watchers in Anubis

City, the whole event lasted less than fifteen minutes. Not until it was all over did anyone pay attention to Europa itself.

The Great Wall was gone: and it was almost an hour before the news came from Earth, Mars, and the Moon that the Sun itself had appeared to flicker for a few seconds, before resuming business as usual.

It had been a highly selective set of eclipses, obviously targeted at humankind. Nowhere else in the Solar System would anything have been noticed.

In the general excitement, it was a little longer before the world realized that TMA-0 and TMA-1 had both vanished, leaving only their four-million-year-old imprints on Tycho and Africa.

It was the first time the Europs could ever have met humans, but they seemed neither alarmed nor surprised by the huge creatures moving among them at such lightning speed. Of course, it was not too easy to interpret the emotional state of something that looked like a small, leafless bush, with no obvious sense organs or means of communication. But if they were frightened by the arrival of *Alcyone,* and the emergence of its passengers, they would surely have remained hiding in their igloos.

As Frank Poole, slightly encumbered by his protective suit and the gift of shining copper wire he was carrying, walked into the untidy suburbs of Tsienville, he wondered what the Europs thought of recent events. For them, there had been no eclipse of Lucifer, but the disappearance of the Great Wall must surely have been a shock. It had stood there from time immemorial, as a shield and doubtless much more; then, abruptly, it was gone, as if it had never been . . .

The petabyte tablet was waiting for him, with a group of Europs standing around it, demonstrating the first sign of curiosity that Poole had ever observed. He wondered if Halman had somehow told them to watch over this gift from space, until he came to collect it.

And to take it back, since it now contained not only a sleeping friend but terrors that some future age might exorcise, to the only place where it could be safely stored.

40. MIDNIGHT: PICO

It would be hard, Poole thought, to imagine a more peaceful scene—especially after the trauma of the last weeks. The slanting rays of a nearly Full Earth revealed all the subtle details of the waterless Sea of Rains—not obliterating them, as the incandescent fury of the Sun would do.

The small convoy of Mooncars was arranged in a semicircle a hundred meters from the inconspicuous opening at the base of Pico that was the entrance to the Vault. From this viewpoint, Poole could see that the mountain did not live up to the name that the early astronomers, misled by its pointed shadow, had given to it. It was more like a rounded hill than a sharp peak, and he could well believe that one of the local pastimes was bicycle-riding to the summit. Until now, none of those sportsmen and women could have guessed at the secret hidden beneath their wheels: he hoped that the sinister knowledge would not discourage their healthy exercise.

An hour ago, with a sense of mingled sadness and triumph, he had handed over the tablet he had brought—never letting it out of his sight—from Ganymede directly to the Moon.

"Goodbye, old friends," he had murmured. "You've done well. Perhaps some future generation will reawaken you. But on the whole—I rather hope not."

He could imagine, all too clearly, one desperate reason why Halman's knowledge might be needed again. By now, surely, some message was on its way to that unknown control center, bearing the news that its servant on Europa no longer existed. With reasonable luck, it would take 950 years, give or take a few, before any response could be expected.

Poole had often cursed Einstein in the past; now he blessed him. Even the powers behind the Monoliths, it now appeared certain, could not spread their influence faster than the speed of light. So the human race should have almost a millennium to prepare for the next encounter—if there was to be one. Perhaps by that time, it would be better prepared.

Something was emerging from the tunnel—the track-mounted, semi-humanoid robot that had carried the tablet into the Vault. It was almost comic to see a machine enclosed in the kind of isolation suit used as protection against deadly germs—and here on the airless Moon! But no one was taking any chances, however unlikely they might seem. After all, the robot had moved among those carefully sequestered nightmares, and although according to its video cameras everything appeared in order, there was always a chance that some vial had leaked, or some canister's seal had broken. The Moon was a very stable environment, but during the centuries it had known many quakes and meteor impacts.

The robot came to a halt, fifty meters outside the tunnel. Slowly, the massive plug that sealed it swung back into place, and began to rotate in its threads, like a giant bolt being screwed into the mountain.

"All not wearing dark glasses, please close your eyes or look away from the robot!" said an urgent voice over the Mooncar radio. Poole twisted round in his seat, just in time to see an explosion of light on the roof of the vehicle. When he turned back to look at Pico, all that was left of the robot was a heap of glowing slag; even to someone who had spent much of his life surrounded by vacuum, it seemed altogether wrong that tendrils of smoke were not slowly spiraling up from it.

"Sterilization completed," said the voice of the Mission Controller. "Thank you, everybody. Now returning to Plato City."

How ironic—that the human race had been saved by the skillful deployment of its own insanities! What moral, Poole wondered, could one possibly draw from that?

He looked back at the beautiful blue Earth, huddling beneath its tattered blanket of clouds for protection against the cold of space. Up there, a few weeks from now, he hoped to cradle his first grandson in his arms.

Whatever godlike powers and principalities lurked beyond the stars,

Poole reminded himself, for ordinary humans only two things were important: Love and Death.

His body had not yet aged a hundred years: he still had plenty of time for both.

EPILOGUE

"Their little universe is very young, and its god is still a child. But it is too soon to judge them; when We return in the Last Days, We will consider what should be saved."

SOURCES AND ACKNOWLEDGMENTS

SOURCES

CHAPTER 1: COMET COWBOY

For a description of Captain Chandler's hunting ground, discovered as recently as 1992, see "The Kuiper Belt" by Jane X. Luu and David C. Jewitt (*Scientific American*, May 1996).

CHAPTER 4: A ROOM WITH A VIEW

The concept of a "ring around the world" in the Geostationary Orbit (GEO), linked to the Earth by towers at the Equator, may seem utterly fantastic but in fact has a firm scientific basis. It is an obvious extension of the "Space Elevator" invented by the St. Petersburg engineer Yuri Artsutanov, whom I had the pleasure of meeting in 1982, when his city had a different name.

Yuri pointed out that it was theoretically possible to lay a cable between the Earth and a satellite hovering over the same spot on the Equator—which it does when placed in the GEO, home of most of today's communications satellites. From this beginning, a Space Elevator (or in Yuri's picturesque phrase, "cosmic funicular") could be established, and payloads could be carried up to the GEO purely by electrical energy. Rocket propulsion would be needed only for the remainder of the journey.

In addition to avoiding the danger, noise, and environmental hazards of rocketry, the space elevator would make possible quite astonishing reductions in the cost of all space missions. Electricity is cheap, and it would require only about a hundred dollars' worth to take one person to orbit. And the round-trip would cost about ten dollars, as most of the energy would be recovered on the downward journey! (Of course, catering and inflight movies would raise the price of the ticket. Would you believe a thousand dollars to GEO and back?)

The theory is impeccable, but does any material exist with sufficient tensile strength to hang all the way down to the Equator from an altitude of 36,000 kilometers, with enough margin left over to raise useful payloads? When Yuri wrote his paper, only one substance met these rather stringent specifications: crystalline carbon, better known as diamond. Unfortunately, the necessary megaton quantities are not readily available on the open market, though in *2061: Odyssey Three* I gave reasons for thinking that they might exist at the core of Jupiter. In *The Fountains of Paradise* I suggested a more accessible source— orbiting factories where diamonds might be grown under zero-gravity conditions.

The first "small step" toward the Space Elevator was attempted in August 1992 on the Shuttle *Atlantis*, when one experiment involved the release—and retrieval—of a payload on a twenty-one-kilometer-long tether. Unfortunately the paying-out mechanism jammed after only a few hundred meters.

I was very flattered when the *Atlantis* crew produced *The Fountains of Paradise* during their orbital press conference, and Mission Specialist Jeffrey Hoffman sent me the autographed copy on their return to Earth.

The second tether experiment, in February 1996, was slightly more successful: the payload was indeed deployed to its full distance, but during retrieval the cable was severed, owing to an electrical discharge caused by faulty insulation. (This may have been a lucky accident: I cannot help recalling that some of Ben Franklin's contemporaries were killed, when they attempted to repeat his famous—and risky— experiment of flying a kite during a thunderstorm.)

Apart from possible dangers, playing out tethered payloads from the Shuttle appears rather like fly-fishing: it is not as easy as it looks. But eventually the final "giant leap" will be made—all the way down to the Equator.

Meanwhile, the discovery of the third form of carbon, buckminsterfullerene (C_{60}) has made the concept of the Space Elevator much more plausible. In 1990 a group of chemists at Rice University, Houston, produced a tubular form of C_{60}—which has far greater tensile strength than diamond. The group's leader, Dr. Smalley, even went so far as to claim it was the strongest material that could ever exist—and added that it would make possible the construction of the Space Elevator. (Stop Press News: I am delighted to know that Dr. Smalley has shared the 1996 Nobel Prize in Chemistry for this work.)

And now for a truly amazing coincidence—one so eerie that it makes me wonder Who Is In Charge.

Buckminister Fuller died in 1983, so never lived to see the discovery of the "buckyballs" and "buckytubes" that have given him much greater posthumous fame. During one of the last of his many world trips, I had the pleasure of flying him and his wife, Anne, around Sri Lanka, and showed them some of the locations featured in *The Fountains of Paradise*. Shortly afterward, I made a recording from the novel on a twelve-inch (remember them?) LP record (Caedmon TC 1606) and Bucky was kind enough to write the sleeve notes. They ended with a surprising revelation, which may well have triggered my own thinking about Star City:

> In 1951 I designed a free-floating tensegrity ring-bridge to be installed way out from and around the Earth's equator. Within this "halo" bridge, the Earth would continue its spinning while the circular bridge would revolve at its own rate. I foresaw Earthian traffic vertically ascending to the bridge, revolving and descending at preferred Earth locii.

I have no doubt that, if the human race decides to make such an investment (a trivial one, according to some estimates of economic growth), Star City could be constructed. In addition to providing new styles of living, and giving visitors from low-gravity worlds like Mars and the Moon better access to the Home Planet, it would eliminate all rocketry from the Earth's surface and relegate it to deep space, where it belongs. (Though I hope there would be occasional anniversary reenactments at Cape Kennedy, to bring back the excitement of the pioneering days.)

Almost certainly most of the City would be empty scaffolding, and only a very small fraction would be occupied or used for scientific or technological purposes. After all, each of the Towers would be the equivalent of a ten-million-floor skyscraper—and the circumference of the ring around the geostationary orbit would be more than half the distance to the Moon! Many times the entire population of the human race could be housed in such a volume of space, if it was all enclosed. (This would pose some interesting logistics problems, which I am content to leave as "an exercise for the student.")

For an excellent history of the "Beanstalk" concept (as well as many other even farther-out ideas such as antigravity and space-warps) see Robert L. Forward's *Indistinguishable from Magic* (Baer, 1995).

CHAPTER 5: EDUCATION

I was astonished to read in the local papers for July 19, 1996, that Dr. Chris Winter, head of British Telecom's Artificial Life Team, believes that the information and storage device I described in this chapter could be developed within thirty years! (In my 1956 novel *The City and the Stars* I put it more than a billion years in the future . . . obviously a serious failure of imagination.) Dr. Winter states that it would allow us to "re-create a person physically, emotionally and spiritually," and estimates that the memory requirements would be about ten terabytes (10e13 bytes), two orders of magnitude less than the petabyte (10e15 bytes) I suggest.

And I wish I'd thought of Dr. Winter's name for this device, which will certainly start some fierce debates in ecclesiastical circles: the "Soul Catcher" . . . For its application to interstellar travel, see note on Chapter 9.

I believed that I had invented the palm-to-palm transfer of information described in Chapter 3, so it was mortifying to discover that Nicholas (*Being Digital*) Negroponte and his MIT Media Lab have been working on the idea for years . . .

CHAPTER 7: DEBRIEFING

If the inconceivable energy of the Zero Point Field (sometimes referred to as "quantum fluctuations" or "vacuum energy") can ever be tapped, the impact upon our civilization will be incalculable. All present sources of power—oil, coal, nuclear, hydro, solar—would become obsolete, and so would many of our fears about environmental pollution. They would all be wrapped up in one big worry—heat pollution. All energy eventually degrades to heat, and if everyone had a few million kilowatts to play with, this planet would soon be heading the way of Venus—several hundred degrees in the shade.

However, there is a bright side to the picture: there may be no other way of averting the next Ice Age, which otherwise is inevitable. ("Civilization is an interval between Ice Ages."—Will Durant, *The Story of Civilization*.)

Even as I write this, many competent engineers, in laboratories all over the world, claim to be tapping this new energy source. Some idea of its magnitude will be given by a famous remark by the physicist Richard Feynman, to the effect that the energy in a coffee mug's volume (any such volume, anywhere!) is enough to boil all the oceans of the world.

This, surely, is a thought to give one pause. By comparison, nuclear energy looks as feeble as a damp match.

And how many super-novae, I wonder, really are industrial accidents?

CHAPTER 9: SKYLAND

One of the main problems of getting around in Star City would be caused by the sheer distances involved: if you wanted to visit a friend in the next Tower (and communications will never completely replace contact, despite all advances in Virtual Reality) it could be the equivalent of a trip to the Moon. Even with the fastest elevators this would involve days rather than hours, or else accelerations quite unacceptable to people who had adapted to low-gravity life.

The concept of an "inertialess drive"—i.e., a propulsion system that acts on every atom of a body so that no strains are produced when it accelerates—was probably invented by the master of the "Space Opera," E. E. Smith, in the 1930s. It is not as improbable as it sounds—because a gravitational field acts in precisely this manner.

If you fall freely near the Earth (neglecting the effects of air resistance) you will increase speed by just under ten meters per second, every second. Yet you will feel weightless—there will be no sense of acceleration, even though your velocity is increasing by one kilometer a second, every minute and a half!

And this would still be true if you were falling in Jupiter's gravity (just over two and a half times Earth's) or even the enormously more powerful field of a white dwarf or neutron star (millions or billions of times greater). You would feel nothing, even if you had approached the velocity of light from a standing start in a matter of minutes.

However, if you were foolish enough to get within a few radii of the attracting object, its field would no longer be uniform over the whole length of your body, and tidal forces would soon tear you to pieces. For further details, see my deplorable but accurately titled short story "Neutron Tide" (in *The Wind from the Sun*).

An "inertialess drive," which would act exactly like a controllable gravity field, had never been discussed seriously outside the pages of science fiction until very recently. But in 1994 three American physicists did exactly this, developing some ideas of the great Russian physicist Andrei Sakharov.

"Inertia as a Zero-Point Field Lorentz Force" by B. Haisch, A. Rueda, and H. E. Puthoff (*Phys Review A*, February 1994) may one day be regarded as a landmark paper, and for the purposes of fiction I have made it so. It addresses a problem so fundamental that it is normally taken for granted, with a "That's just the way the universe is made" shrug of the shoulders.

The question HR&P asked is: "What gives an object mass (or inertia) so that it requires an effort to start it moving, and exactly the same effort to restore it to its original state?"

Their provisional answer depends on the astonishing and—outside the physicists' ivory towers—little-known fact that so-called empty space is actually a cauldron of seething energies—the Zero Point Field (see note above). HR&P suggest that both inertia and gravitation are electromagnetic phenomena, resulting from interaction with this field.

There have been countless attempts, going all the way back to Faraday, to link gravity and magnetism, and although many experimenters have claimed success, none of their results has ever been verified. However, if HR&P's theory can be proved, it opens up the prospect—however remote—of anti-gravity "space drives," and the even more fantastic possibility of controlling inertia. This could lead to some interesting situations: if you gave someone the gentlest touch, they would promptly disappear at thousands of kilometers an hour, until they bounced off the other side of the room a fraction of a millisecond later. The good news is that traffic accidents would be virtually impossible; automobiles—and passengers—could collide harmlessly at any speed. (And you think that today's lifestyles are already too hectic?)

The "weightlessness" that we now take for granted in space missions—and which millions of tourists will be enjoying in the next century—would have seemed like magic to our grandparents. But the abolition—or merely the reduction—of inertia is quite another matter, and may be completely impossible.* But it's a nice thought, for it could provide the equivalent of "teleportation": you could travel anywhere (at least on Earth) almost instantaneously. Frankly, I don't know how "Star City" could manage without it . . .

One of the assumptions I have made in this novel is that Einstein is correct, and that no signal—or object—can exceed the speed of light. A number of highly mathematical papers have recently appeared suggesting that, as countless science-fiction writers have taken for granted, galactic hitchhikers may not have to suffer this annoying restriction.

On the whole, I hope they are right—but there seems one fundamental objection. If FTL is possible, where are all those hitchhikers—or at least the well-heeled tourists?

One answer is that no sensible ETs will ever build interstellar vehicles, for precisely the same reason that we have never developed coal-fueled airships: there are much better ways of doing the job.

The surprisingly small number of "bits" required to define a human being, or to store all the information one could possibly acquire in a lifetime, is discussed in "Machine Intelligence, the Cost of Interstellar Travel and Fermi's Paradox" by Louis K. Scheffer (*Quarterly Journal of the Royal Astronomical Society* 35, no. 2 [June 1994]: 157–175). This paper (surely the most mind-stretching that the staid *QJRAS* has published in its entire career!) estimates that the total mental state of a one-hundred-year-old human with a perfect memory could be represented by ten to the fifteenth bits (one petabit). Even today's optical fibers could transmit this amount of information in a matter of minutes.

My suggestion that a *Star Trek* transporter would still be unavailable in 3001 may therefore appear ludicrously shortsighted a mere century from now, and the present lack of interstellar tourists is simply due to the fact that no receiving equipment has yet been set up on Earth. Perhaps it's already on its way by slow boat . . .

---

* In September 1996, scientists in Finland claimed to have detected a small (less than 1 percent) reduction in gravity above a spinning, superconducting disk. If this is confirmed (and apparently earlier experiments at Munich's Max Planck Institute have hinted at similar results) it might be the long-awaited breakthrough. I await further news with interested skepticism.

CHAPTER 15: TRANSIT OF VENUS

It gives me particular pleasure to pay this tribute to the crew of *Apollo 15*. On their return from the Moon they sent me the beautiful relief map of the Lunar Module *Falcon*'s landing site, which now has pride of place in my office. It shows the routes taken by the Lunar Rover during its three excursions, one of which skirted Earthlight crater. The map bears the inscription: "To Arthur Clarke from the crew of *Apollo 15* with many thanks for your visions of space. Dave Scott, Al Worden, Jim Irwin." In return, I have now dedicated *Earthlight* (which, written in 1953, was set in the territory the Rover was to drive over in 1971) "To Dave Scott and Jim Irwin, the first men to enter this land, and to Al Worden, who watched over them from orbit."

After covering the *Apollo 15* landing in the CBS studio with Walter Cronkite and Wally Schirra, I flew to Mission Control to watch the reentry and splashdown. I was sitting beside Al Worden's little daughter when she was the first to notice that one of the capsule's three parachutes had failed to deploy. It was a tense moment, but luckily the remaining two were quite adequate for the job.

CHAPTER 16: THE CAPTAIN'S TABLE

See Chapter 18 of *2001: A Space Odyssey* for the description of the probe's impact. Precisely such an experiment is now being planned for the forthcoming Clementine 2 mission.

I am a little embarrassed to see that in my first *Space Odyssey* the discovery of Asteroid 7794 was attributed to the Lunar Observatory—in 1997! Well, I'll move it to 2017—in time for my one hundredth birthday.

Just a few hours after writing the above, I was delighted to learn that Asteroid 4923 (1981 EO27), discovered by S. J. Bus at Siding Spring, Australia, on March 2, 1981, has been named Clarke, partly in recognition of Project Spaceguard (see *Rendezvous with Rama* and *The Hammer of God*). I was informed, with profound apologies, that owing to an unfortunate oversight, Number 2001 was no longer available, having been allocated to somebody named A. Einstein. Excuses, excuses . . .

But I was very pleased to learn that Asteroid 5020, discovered on the same day as 4923, has been named Asimov—though saddened by the fact that my old friend could never know.

CHAPTER 17: GANYMEDE

As explained in the Valediction, and in the "Author's Notes" to *2010: Odyssey Two* and *2061: Odyssey Three*, I had hoped that the ambitious Galileo Mission to Jupiter and its moons would by now have given us much more detailed knowledge—as well as stunning close-ups—of these strange worlds.

Well, after many delays, *Galileo* reached its first objective—Jupiter itself—and is performing admirably. But, alas, there is a problem—for some reason, the main antenna never unfolded. This means that images have to be sent back via a low-gain antenna, at an agonizingly slow rate. Although miracles of onboard computer reprogramming have been done to compensate for this, it will still require hours to receive information that should have been sent in minutes.

So we must be patient—and I was in the tantalizing position of exploring Ganymede in fiction, just before *Galileo* started to do so in reality, on June 27, 1996.

On July 11, 1996, just two days before finishing this book, I downloaded the first images from JPL; luckily nothing—so far!—contradicts my descriptions. But if the current vistas of cratered ice-fields suddenly give way to palm trees and tropical beaches—or, worse still, YANKEE GO HOME signs—I'll be in real trouble . . .

I am particularly looking forward to close-ups of "Ganymede City" (Chapter 17). This striking formation is exactly as I described it—though I hesitated to do so for fear that my "discovery" might be front-paged by the *National Prevaricator*. To my eyes it appears considerably more artificial than the notorious "Mars Face" and its surroundings. And if its streets and avenues are ten kilometers wide—so what? Perhaps the Medes were BIG . . .

The city will be found on the NASA *Voyager* images 20637.02 and 20637.29, or more conveniently in Figure 23.8 of John H. Rogers's monumental *The Giant Planet Jupiter* (Cambridge University Press, 1995).

CHAPTER 19: THE MADNESS OF MANKIND

For visual evidence supporting Khan's startling assertion that most of mankind has been at least partially insane, see Episode 22, "Meeting Mary," in my television series *Arthur C. Clarke's Mysterious Universe*. And bear in mind that Christians represent only a very small subset of our species: far greater numbers of devotees than those who have ever worshipped the Virgin Mary have given equal reverence to such totally incompatible divinities as Rama, Kali, Siva, Thor, Wotan, Jupiter, Osiris, etc., etc. . . .

The most striking—and pitiful—example of a brilliant man whose beliefs turned him into a raving lunatic is that of Conan Doyle. Despite endless exposures of his favorite psychics as frauds, his faith in them remained unshaken. And the creator of Sherlock Holmes even tried to convince the great magician Harry Houdini that he "dematerialized" himself to perform his feats of escapology—often based on tricks that, as Dr. Watson was fond of saying, were "absurdly simple." (See the essay "The Irrelevance of Conan Doyle" in Martin Gardner's *The Night Is Large*.)

For details of the Inquisition, whose pious atrocities make Pol Pot and the Nazis look positively benign, see Carl Sagan's devastating attack on New Age Nitwittery, *The Demon-Haunted World*. I wish it— and Martin's book—could be made required reading in every high school and college.

At least the U.S. Department of Immigration has taken action against one religion-inspired barbarity. *Time* magazine ("Milestones," June 24, 1996) reports that asylum must now be granted to girls threatened with genital mutilation in their countries of origin.

I had already written this chapter when I came across Anthony Storr's *Feet of Clay: The Power and Charisma of Gurus* (The Free Press, 1996), which is a virtual textbook on this depressing subject. It is hard to believe that one holy fraud, by the time the U.S. Marshals belatedly arrested him, had accumulated ninety-three Rolls-Royces! Even worse—83 percent of his thousands of American dupes had been to college, and thus qualify for my favorite definition of an intellectual: "Someone who has been educated beyond his/her intelligence."

CHAPTER 26: TSIENVILLE

In the 1982 preface to *2010: Odyssey Two*, I explained why I named the Chinese spaceship that landed on Europa after Dr. Tsien Hsue-shen, one of the founders of the United States and Chinese rocket programs.

Born in 1911, Tsien won a scholarship that brought him from China to the United States in 1935, where he became student and later colleague of the brilliant Hungarian aerodynamicist Theodore von Karman. Later, as first Goddard Professor at the California Institute of Technology, he helped establish the Guggenheim Aeronautical

Laboratory—the direct ancestor of Pasadena's famed Jet Propulsion Laboratory. As the *New York Times* (October 28, 1966) commented ("Peking Rocket Chief Was Trained in U.S.") just after China conducted a guided-missile nuclear weapons test over its own territory, "Tsien's life is an irony of Cold War history."

With top-secret clearance, he contributed greatly to American rocket research in the 1950s, but during the hysteria of the McCarthy era was arrested on trumped-up security charges when he attempted to pay a visit to his native China. After many hearings and a prolonged period of arrest, he was finally deported to his homeland—with all his unrivaled knowledge and expertise. As many of his distinguished colleagues affirmed, it was one of the most stupid (as well as most disgraceful) things the United States ever did.

After his expulsion, according to Zhuang Fenggan, Deputy Director, Science and Technology Committee, China National Space Administration, Tsien "started the rocket business from nothing . . . Without him, China would have suffered a twenty-year lag in technology." And a corresponding delay, perhaps, in the deployment of the deadly "Silkworm" antiship missile and the "Long March" satellite launcher.

Shortly after I had completed this novel, the International Academy of Astronautics honored me with its highest distinction, the von Karman Award—to be given in Beijing! This was an offer I couldn't refuse, especially when I learned that Dr. Tsien is now a resident of that city. Unfortunately, when I arrived there I discovered that he was in the hospital for observation, and his doctors whould not permit visitors.

I am therefore extremely grateful to his personal assistant, Major-General Wang Shouyun, for carrying suitably inscribed copies of *2010* and *2061* to Dr. Tsien. In return the General presented me with the massive volume he has edited, *Collected Works of H. S. Tsien: 1938–1956* (Science Press, 16, Donghuangcheggen North Street, Beijing 100707, 1991). It is a fascinating collection, beginning with numerous collaborations with von Karman on problems in aerodynamics, and ending with solo papers on rockets and satellites. The very last entry, "Thermonuclear Power Plants" (*Jet Propulsion*, July 1956), was written while Dr. Tsien was still a virtual prisoner of the FBI, and deals with a subject that is even more topical today—though very little progress has been made toward "a power station utilizing the deuterium fusion reaction."

Just before I left Beijing on October 13, 1996, I was happy to learn that, despite his current age (eighty-five) and disability, Dr. Tsien is still pursuing his scientific studies. I sincerely hope that he enjoyed *2010* and *2061* and look forward to sending him this *Final Odyssey* as an additional tribute.

CHAPTER 36: CHAMBER OF HORRORS

As the result of a series of Senate Hearings on Computer Security in June 1996, on July 15, 1996, President Clinton signed Executive Order 13010 to deal with "computer-based attacks on the information or communications components that control critical infrastructures ('cyber threats')." This will set up a task force to counter cyberterrorism, and will have representatives from the CIA, NSA, defense agencies, etc.

Pico, here we come . . .

Since writing the above paragraph, I have been intrigued to learn that the finale of *Independence Day*, which I have not yet seen, also involves the use of computer viruses as Trojan horses! I am also informed that its opening is identical to that of *Childhood's End* (1953), and that it contains every known science-fiction cliché since Melies' *Trip to the Moon* (1903).

I cannot decide whether to congratulate the scriptwriters on their one stroke of originality—or to accuse them of the trans-temporal crime of precognitive plagiarism. In any event, I fear there's nothing I can do to stop John Q. Popcorn thinking that I have ripped off the ending of *ID4*.

The following material has been taken—usually with major editing—from the earlier books in the series:

From *2001: A Space Odyssey*: Chapter 18, "Through the Asteroids"; and Chapter 37, "Experiment."

From *2010: Odyssey Two*: Chapter 11, "Ice and Vacuum"; Chapter 36, "Fire in the Deep"; Chapter 38, "Foamscape."

ACKNOWLEDGMENTS

My thanks to IBM for presenting me with the beautiful little Thinkpad 755CD on which this book was composed. For many years I have been embarrassed by the—totally unfounded—rumor that the name HAL was derived by one letter displacement from IBM. In an attempt to exorcise this computer-age myth, I even went to the trouble of getting Dr. Chandra, HAL's inventor, to deny it in *2010: Odyssey Two*. However, I was recently assured that, far from being annoyed by the association, Big Blue is now quite proud of it. So I will abandon any future attempts to put the record straight—and send my congratulations to all those participating in HAL's "birthday party" at (of course) the University of Illinois, Urbana, on March 12, 1997.

Rueful gratitude to my Del Rey Books editor, Shelly Shapiro, for ten pages of niggles that, when dealt with, made a vast improvement to the final product. (Yes, I've been an editor myself, and do not suffer from the usual author's conviction that the members of this trade are frustrated butchers.)

Finally, and most important of all: my deepest thanks to my old friend Cyril Gardiner, Chairman of the Galle Face Hotel, for the hospitality of his magnificent (and enormous) personal suite while I was writing this book: he gave me a Tranquillity Base in a time of troubles. I hasten to add that, even though it may not provide such extensive imaginary landscapes, the facilities of the Galle Face are far superior to those offered by the "Grannymede," and never in my life have I worked in more comfortable surroundings.

Or, for that matter, in more inspirational ones, for a large plaque at the entrance lists more than a hundred of the Heads of State and other distinguished visitors who have been entertained here. They include Yuri Gagarin, the crew of *Apollo 12*—the second mission to the Moon's surface—and a fine collection of stage and movie stars: Gregory Peck, Alec Guinness, Noel Coward, *Star Wars'* Carrie Fisher . . . As well as Vivien Leigh and Laurence Olivier—both of whom make brief appearances in *2061: Odyssey Three* (Chapter 37). I am honored to see my name listed among them.

It seems appropriate that a project begun in one famous hotel—
New York's Chelsea, that hotbed of genuine and imitation genius—
should be concluded in another, half a world away. But it's strange to
hear the monsoon-lashed Indian Ocean roaring just a few yards outside my window, instead of the traffic along far-off and fondly remembered 23rd Street.

IN MEMORIAM: SEPTEMBER 18, 1996
It was with the deepest regret that I heard—literally while
editing these acknowledgments—that Cyril Gardiner died
a few hours ago.

It is some consolation to know that he had already seen
the above tribute, and was delighted with it.

VALEDICTION

"Never explain, never apologize" may be excellent advice for politicians, Hollywood moguls, and business tycoons, but an author should treat his readers with more consideration. So, though I have no intention of apologizing for anything, perhaps the complicated genesis of the *Odyssey* Quartet requires a little explaining.

It all began at Christmas 1948—yes, 1948!—with a four-thousand-word short story that I wrote for a contest sponsored by the British Broadcasting Corporation. "The Sentinel" described the discovery of a small pyramid on the Moon, set there by some alien civilization to await the emergence of mankind as a planet-faring species. Until then, it was implied, we would be too primitive to be of any interest.*

The BBC rejected my modest effort, and it was not published until almost three years later in the one-and-only (Spring 1951) issue of *10 Story Fantasy*—a magazine that, as the invaluable *Encyclopedia of Science Fiction* wryly comments, is "primarily remembered for its poor arithmetic (there were thirteen stories)."

"The Sentinel" remained in limbo for more than a decade, until Stanley Kubrick contacted me in the spring of 1964 and asked if I had any ideas for the "proverbial" (i.e., still nonexistent) "good science

---

* The search for alien artifacts in the Solar System should be a perfectly legitimate branch of science ("exo-archaeology"?). Unfortunately it has been largely discredited by claims that such evidence has already been found—and has been deliberately suppressed by NASA! It is incredible that anyone would believe such nonsense: far more likely that the space agency would deliberately fake ET artifacts—to solve its budget problems! (Over to you, NASA Administrator . . .)

fiction movie." During the course of our many brainstorming sessions, as recounted in *The Lost Worlds of 2001*, we decided that the patient watcher on the Moon might provide a good starting point for our story. Eventually it did much more than that, as somewhere during production the pyramid evolved into the now famous black Monolith.

To put the *Odyssey* series in perspective, it must be remembered that when Stanley and I started planning what we privately called "How the Solar System Was Won" the Space Age was barely seven years old, and no human had traveled more than a hundred kilometers from the home planet. Although President Kennedy had announced that the United States intended to go to the Moon "in this decade," to most people that must still have seemed like a far-off dream. When filming started in South London* on a freezing December 29, 1965, we did not even know what the lunar surface looked like at close quarters. There were still fears that the first word uttered by an emerging astronaut would be "Help!" as he disappeared into a talcum-powder-like layer of moondust. On the whole, we guessed fairly well: only the fact that our lunar landscapes are more jagged than the real ones—smoothed by aeons of sandblasting by meteoric dust—reveals that *2001* was made in the pre-*Apollo* era.

Today, of course, it seems ludicrous that we could have imagined giant space stations, orbiting Hilton Hotels, and expeditions to Jupiter as early as 2001. It is now difficult to realize that back in the 1960s there were serious plans for permanent Moon bases and Mars landings—by 1990! Indeed, in the CBS studio, immediately after the *Apollo 11* launch, I heard the Vice President of the United States proclaim exuberantly: "Now we must go to Mars!"

As it turned out, he was lucky not to go to prison. That scandal, plus Vietnam and Watergate, is one of the reasons why these optimistic scenarios never materialized.

When the movie and book of *2001: A Space Odyssey* made their appearance in 1968, the possibility of a sequel had never crossed my mind. But in 1979 a mission to Jupiter really did take place, and we obtained our first close-ups of the giant planet and its astonishing family of moons.

The *Voyager* space-probes† were, of course, unmanned, but the im-

---

* At Shepperton, destroyed by the Martians in one of the most dramatic scenes in Wells's masterpiece, *The War of the Worlds*.

† Which employed a "slingshot" or "gravity-assist" maneuver by flying close to Jupiter—precisely as was done by *Discovery* in the book version of *2001*.

ages they sent back made real—and totally unexpected—worlds from what had hitherto been merely points of light in the most powerful telescopes. The continually erupting sulfur volcanoes of Io, the multiply-impacted face of Callisto, the weirdly contoured landscape of Ganymede—it was almost as if we had discovered a whole new Solar System. The temptation to explore it was irresistible, hence *2010: Odyssey Two*, which also gave me the opportunity to find out what happened to David Bowman, after he had awakened in that enigmatic hotel room.

In 1981, when I started writing the new book, the Cold War was still in progress, and I felt I was going out on a limb—as well as risking criticism—by showing a joint U.S.-Russian mission. I also underlined my hope of future cooperation by dedicating the novel to Nobelist Andrei Sakharov (then still in exile) and Cosmonaut Alexei Leonov—who, when I told him in "Star Village" that the ship would be named after him, exclaimed with typical ebullience, "Then it will be a good ship!"

It still seems incredible to me that, when Peter Hyams made his excellent film version in 1983, he was able to use the actual close-ups of the Jovian moons obtained in the *Voyager* missions (some of them after helpful computer processing by the Jet Propulsion Laboratory, source of the originals). However, far better images were expected from the ambitious *Galileo* mission, due to carry out a detailed survey of the major satellites over a period of many months. Our knowledge of this new territory, previously obtained only from a brief flyby, would be enormously expanded—and I would have no excuse for not writing *Odyssey Three*.

Alas—something tragic on the way to Jupiter. It had been planned to launch *Galileo* from the Space Shuttle in 1986—but the *Challenger* disaster ruled out that option, and it soon became clear that we would get no new information from Io and Europa, Ganymede and Callisto, for at least another decade.

I decided not to wait, and the (1985) return of Halley's Comet to the inner Solar System gave me an irresistible theme. Its next appearance in 2061 would be good timing for a third *Odyssey*, though as I was not certain when I could deliver it I asked my publisher for a rather modest advance. It is with much sadness that I quote the dedication of *2061: Odyssey Three*:

To the memory of
Judy-Lynn del Rey,
editor extraordinary,
who bought this book for one dollar
—but never knew if she got her money's worth

Obviously there is no way in which a series of four science fiction novels, written over a period of more than thirty years of the most breathtaking developments in technology (especially in space exploration) and politics could be mutually consistent. As I wrote in the introduction to *2061*, "Just as *2010: Odyssey Two* was not a direct sequel to *2001: A Space Odyssey*, so this book is not a linear sequel to *2010*. They must all be considered as variations on the same theme, involving many of the same characters and situations, but not necessarily happening in the same universe." If you want a good analogy from another medium, listen to what Rachmaninoff and Andrew Lloyd Webber did to the same handful of notes by Paganini.

So this *Final Odyssey* has discarded many of the elements of its precursors, but developed others—and I hope more important ones—in much greater detail. And if any readers of the earlier books feel disoriented by such transmutations, I hope I can dissuade them from sending me angry letters of denunciation by adapting one of the more endearing remarks of a certain U.S. President: "It's fiction, stupid!"

And it's all my own fiction, in case you hadn't noticed. Though I have much enjoyed my collaborations with Gentry Lee,* Michael Kube-McDowell, and the late Mike McQuay—and won't hesitate again to call on the best hired guns in the business if I have future projects that are too big to handle myself—this particular *Odyssey* had to be a solo job.

So every word is mine: well, almost every word. I must confess that I found Professor Thirugnanasampanthamoorthy (Chapter 35) in the Colombo telephone directory; I hope the present owner of that name will not object to the loan. There are also a few borrowings from the great *Oxford English Dictionary*. And what do you know—to my delighted surprise, I find it uses no less than sixty-six quotations from my own books to illustrate the meaning and use of words!

---

* By an unlikely coincidence, Gentry was Chief Engineer on the *Galileo* and *Viking* projects. (See Introduction to *Rama II*.) It wasn't his fault that the *Galileo* antenna didn't unfurl . . .

Dear *OED*, if you find any useful examples in these pages, please be my guest—again.

I apologize for the number of modest coughs (about ten, at last count) in this Afterword; but the matters to which they drew attention seemed too relevant to be omitted.

Finally, I would like to assure my many Buddhist, Christian, Hindu, Jewish, and Muslim friends that I am sincerely happy that the religion which Chance has given you has contributed to your peace of mind (and often, as Western medical science now reluctantly admits, to your physical well-being).

Perhaps it is better to be un-sane and happy, than sane and unhappy. But it is best of all to be sane and happy.

Whether our descendants can achieve that goal will be the greatest challenge of the future. Indeed, it may well decide whether we have any future.

Arthur C. Clarke
Colombo, Sri Lanka
September 19, 1996

ARTHUR C. CLARKE was born in Minehead, England, in 1917 and was made a Freeman of his hometown in 1992. He now lives in Sri Lanka, where he was the first person to be granted "Resident Guest" status. He is a graduate, and Fellow, of King's College, London, and Chancellor of the International Space University and the University of Moratuwa, near which the Government has established the Arthur C. Clarke Centre for Modern Technologies.

Dr. Clarke has twice been Chairman of the British Interplanetary Society. While serving as an RAF radar officer in 1945, he published the theory of communications satellites, most of which operate in what is now called the Clarke Orbit. The impact of this invention upon global politics resulted in his nomination for the 1994 Nobel Peace Prize.

He has written over seventy books, and he shared an Oscar nomination with Stanley Kubrick for the movie based on his novel *2001: A Space Odyssey*. His *Mysterious World, Strange Powers*, and *Mysterious Universe* TV series have been shown worldwide.

His many honors include the Marconi and Lindbergh Awards, as well as three Hugos and three Nebulas for his science fiction. In a global satellite ceremony in 1995, he received NASA's highest civilian honor, its Distinguished Public Service Medal.

Dr. Clarke's recreations are scuba diving on Indian Ocean wrecks with his company, Underwater Safaris, table tennis (despite Post Polio Syndrome), observing the Moon through his fourteen-inch telescope, and playing with his Chihuahua, "Pepsi," and his six computers.

He received the Vidya Jyothi ("Light of Science") Award from the president of Sri Lanka in 1986, and the CBE (Commander of the British Empire) from H.M. Queen Elizabeth in 1989. And in 1996 he went to Beijing to receive the International Academy of Astronautics' highest honor, the von Karman Award.